MICAH'S SUPER VLOG!

TO SKETCH A THIEF

ALSO AVAILABLE:

MICAH'S SUPER VLOG! TO SKETCH A THIEF

BY **ANDY MCGUIRE**

ILLUSTRATIONS BY **GIRISH MANUEL**

Copyright ©2019 by Hachette Book Group, Inc.

Published in association with minno kids™

Cover copyright ©2019 by Hachette Book Group, Inc.

FaithWords is a division of Hachette Book Group, Inc. The FaithWords name and logo are trademarks of Hachette Book Group, Inc.

FaithWords
Hachette Book Group
1290 Avenue of the Americas, New York, NY 10104

hachettebookgroup.com | faithwords.com | gominno.com

Micah's Super Vlog was created by Girish Manuel. Micah's Super Vlog trademark and character rights are owned by Square One World Media, Inc., and used by permission.

Written by Andy McGuire
Illustrated by Girish Manuel and Stu Hunnable

Scripture quotations marked (NLT) are taken from the Holy Bible, New Living Translation, copyright ©1996, 2004, 2015 by Tyndale House Foundation. Used by permission of Tyndale House Publishers, Inc., Carol Stream, Illinois 60188. All rights reserved.

Scripture quotations marked (CEV) are from the Contemporary English Version Copyright © 1991, 1992, 1995 by American Bible Society. Used by permission.

Scripture quotations marked (ESV) are from the ESV® Bible (The Holy Bible, English Standard Version®), copyright © 2001 by Crossway, a publishing ministry of Good News Publishers. Used by permission. All rights reserved.

Scripture quotations marked (ICB) are from the International Children's Bible®. Copyright © 1986, 1988, 1999 by Thomas Nelson. Used by permission. All rights reserved.

Scripture quotations marked (NIV) are taken from the Holy Bible, New International Version®, NIV®. Copyright © 1973, 1978, 1984, 2011 by Biblica, Inc.™ Used by permission of Zondervan. All rights reserved worldwide. www.zondervan.com The "NIV" and "New International Version" are trademarks registered in the United States Patent and Trademark Office by Biblica, Inc.™

First Edition: October 2019

Library of Congress Cataloging-in-Publication Data has been applied for.

ISBN: 978-1-5460-2657-0 (trade paperback), 978-1-5460-2656-3 (ebook)

Printed in the USA.
LSC-C
10 9 8 7 6 5 4 3 2 1

To Jane, the first and most frequent reader of my books,
and the one most likely to quote me back to myself
—for better or worse. I love you.
—AM

To Stu, who's helped me make Micah's Super Vlog from the
very beginning, even when you lived across the pond!
—GM

CHAPTER ONE

There's nothing quite like the feeling of being an actor in a play. The rush of pretending to be someone else, taking on his personality, his hopes, his dreams. In fact, it can quickly become so much more than just pretending—you put on that costume and makeup, and it becomes easy to think like your character, act like your character, and talk like your character. You are completely transformed! It's almost like magic, the way you forget who you are and become someone else!

Unless your character is an artichoke. Then you just feel like a fifth grader in a weird costume.

Backstage in the New Leaf Elementary School auditorium, Micah Murphy was all dressed up but having trouble completely transforming. He was green, round, and bumpy from head to toe, exactly the way he was supposed to be, but he just wasn't feeling it. He had no idea how to think, act, or talk like an "edible thistle" (which was what he learned an "artichoke" was when he looked it up in the school library dictionary).

No, he was still just plain old Micah. And that wasn't very exciting.

He wasn't sure why he wasn't feeling it. He'd actually been excited to try out for Miss Petunia's latest food-based musical, *Don't You Carrot All?* Normally he had to be tricked into being in one of her strange productions, but this time he went into it with eyes wide-open. Ever since Micah's recent gig as a Middletown tour guide, dressed up in a historical costume, he'd come to realize there was a small part of him that actually enjoyed acting, and even being in front of a crowd. Besides, all his friends were in the musical, and who wants to hang out by yourself after school?

It was dark backstage, so it was hard at first for Micah to tell that it was Lydia coming toward him from stage left. She was wearing an enormous cardboard bowl filled with chunky gray Styrofoam.

"What are you supposed to be?" Micah asked.

"Cream of mushroom soup."

"I would've guessed clam chowder."

"There's no clam chowder in this play."

"Oh. I haven't read the script yet."

One of Micah's other friends, Armin, came in through a side door and joined them. He was dressed in a red rectangular box with small, black wads of construction paper coming out the top. "Did I really just hear you say you haven't read the script yet, Micah?"

"Not the whole thing. I read my lines at the tryout. I just didn't read anything else."

"How did you know what part to try out for?" Lydia asked.

"Miss Petunia said I had 'artichoke' written all over me."

Armin looked him up and down and shrugged. "I can see that."

Micah looked Armin up and down in return. "What are you supposed to be?"

"A box of raisins."

"Makes sense."

"Does it?" Armin asked.

Micah wasn't sure how to answer this, so he asked a question of his own. "Does it seem weird that we're wearing our costumes on the first day of rehearsal?"

Lydia shook her head. "This is always Miss Petunia's process. She believes the costumes make us embody the characters."

Suddenly, one of Micah's other friends, Gabe, wriggled across the floor in front of them. He was dressed in a huge, red sleeping bag with holes cut out for his arms and legs. There was no hole cut out for his head. He didn't say a word as he twisted himself around a corner and out of sight.

"I think he's a gummy worm," Armin said.

Micah shrugged. "I haven't figured out what this play is about yet, other than weird foods."

"It's about how certain kinds of foods like to hang out together," Armin said, "like in a soup or in a salad. But other foods always feel left out."

Lydia nodded. "For instance, in scene 2 the bananas want to be in an omelet, but the eggs won't let them. And the cantaloupe and M&M's

want to be included on submarine sandwiches, but the bread won't let them."

"My mom would love this play!" Micah said. "Whenever I tell her something sounds gross and I don't want to eat it, she's always telling me, 'You never know if it's good until you've tried it!'"

"Actually," Lydia answered, "the play is a brilliant commentary on modern relationships and how we're reluctant to trust others in an age of social isolation."

"Um . . . what was that, now?"

"I think she means it's about how to be a good friend," said Armin.

"Oh," said Micah. "Sounds . . . interesting, I guess."

Gabe slithered back around the corner, then wriggled his way across the back of the stage and out of sight behind a curtain.

Thump! Bump, bump, bump, bump, bump. Bang!

"Did Gabe know there's a staircase back there?" Micah asked.

"I think he does now," Lydia said.

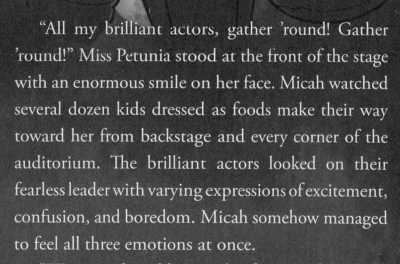

"All my brilliant actors, gather 'round! Gather 'round!" Miss Petunia stood at the front of the stage with an enormous smile on her face. Micah watched several dozen kids dressed as foods make their way toward her from backstage and every corner of the auditorium. The brilliant actors looked on their fearless leader with varying expressions of excitement, confusion, and boredom. Micah somehow managed to feel all three emotions at once.

"We are gathered here today for one of the most exciting moments of my teaching career!" Miss

Petunia said. "We are ready to start rehearsing *Don't You Carrot All?*—an incredible musical I've been longing to direct all my life!"

"Didn't she write it herself?" Armin whispered to Micah and Lydia.

"And I think she just finished it last week," Lydia added.

Miss Petunia cleared her throat to get their attention and went on. "It's a food-based production, which you've all grown to love and appreciate. But what you may not know is it's the first vegetarian musical ever performed on American soil. My brilliant actors: we are about to make history!"

A first grader dressed as a pineapple raised her hand. "What's vegetarian?"

Miss Petunia looked surprised by the question, but no less enthusiastic. "It means someone who doesn't eat meat."

"But how could a musical eat meat?" a third-grade turnip asked.

"Musicals don't eat anything," Miss Petunia said.

Some of the Food-Based Musicals Miss Petunia Has Written and Directed

- Something to Taco 'Bout
- Lettuce Play Too!
- Born and Bread
- What's at Steak?
- Honeydew You Love Me?
- Give Peas a Chance
- How Waffle That Feels
- Plum Out of Ideas

Something to TACO 'BOUT!

How Waffle That feels?

"What I meant to say is that there is no meat in this musical."

"So it's the first musical without any meat in it?" asked a second-grade box of macaroni.

"I don't remember any meat in *The Music Man*," said a lime Jell-O mold.

"No . . . I just meant—" Miss Petunia started.

Mercifully, she was saved by the banging of the double doors in the back of the auditorium as they flew open. Small people dressed in strange colors and shapes rushed toward the stage, followed closely by a large fifth grader on a scooter.

The boy on the scooter weaved in and out of the small people as they headed forward, keeping them in a tight circle until, racing all the way to the foot of the stage, they fell over each other in a large heap. They looked like a load of laundry someone dropped on the floor before folding it.

"Thank you, Chet," said Miss Petunia to the boy on the scooter.

Beads of sweat rolled down Chet's face. "Whew!

Herding kindergartners is hard work! What are they supposed to be, anyway?"

"They're my vegetable soup! Carrots. Onions. Tomatoes. Kale. Et cetera," Miss Petunia answered in an excited trill. "I knew the kindergartners would wander over to the playground after they got their costumes on. Chet, you did an admirable job gathering them back, and now you're free to go home from detention. Unless you want to be in my musical too!"

Chet scootered out of there so fast you could almost see blurry lines behind him, like in a cartoon.

Miss Petunia looked around at her actors. "You've all had the opportunity to read the script by now. Are there any questions about the musical? Anything that doesn't make sense?"

Every hand in the auditorium shot up.

The smile on Miss Petunia's face remained unchanged. "On second thought, perhaps you'll understand it better once we begin rehearsing."

Micah walked into the boys' changing room after rehearsal to take his costume off. Hanz, an exchange student from Germany and one of Micah's least-favorite fifth graders, was already in there. He was half-dressed in a long, green tube of felt. He looked Micah up and down, from the lumpy felt hat on his head all the way to the green galoshes on his feet. "So, vat are you supposed to be, anyvay? You look like somezing my cat coughed up."

"I'm an artichoke," said Micah. "What are you?"

"I am ze lead celery. No other celery has more lines zan me—"

"You're the only celery," Armin cut in, pulling the raisin box over his head.

Hanz handed his script to Micah and Armin to look at. Sure enough, it said "lead celery" on the top. In pencil. In Hanz's own handwriting.

Micah rolled his eyes. His artichoke costume was hard to pull over his head, but he had finally shimmied his way out of it with both ears intact.

"Hey!" Armin suddenly shouted. "Someone stole

my sketchbook!" Other kids, who had been milling about in and out of the changing room, stopped what they were doing.

"Vat sketchbook?" Hanz asked.

"My sketchbook," Armin said. "I left it right here beside my backpack! I had all my best pictures in there. There was a drawing of my cat that I shaded so carefully, you'd have thought it was in 3-D!"

"Everybody should check and see if anything else is missing," said Frank Millwood, the most popular boy in all of fifth grade. Unlike Hanz, Frank really was the lead in the musical—he was a loaf of French bread, with nearly forty lines. And some of them were actually in French!

"Nothing missing from me!" said PB, in the form of a spinach leaf. "I never lose things." PB was one of the school's two student news correspondents. He and his partner, J, had an afternoon news show that was broadcast to every classroom at New Leaf Elementary.

"Or me!" said Liam Paval, a third-grade lasagna noodle.

"Or me!" said Eric Lakota, a fourth-grade slice of cheddar.

One by one, everybody confirmed that the only thing that had disappeared was Armin's sketchbook. But why? And even more important: Who took it?

Suddenly Armin shouted: "Chet!"

A Sketchy Situation

I can't believe someone stole Armin's sketchbook! Who would do that? I know we have some mean kids in this school—Chet and Hanz come to mind, of course—but who would mess with Armin like that? He's one of the nicest kids in school!

We need to investigate. Who are the key subjects? What's the motive? Where was Armin's sketchbook last seen? Actually, this might be kind of fun! It'll be just like those cop TV shows. Maybe I should write myself a theme song!

But that can probably wait. Between the musical and detecting (that's what detectives do, right?), it's going to be crazy around here for a while! All I know is, I need to have Armin's back. He'd definitely help me out if the shoe was on the other foot.

A friend is always loyal, and a brother is born to help in time of need.
Proverbs 17:17 (NLT)

▷ **What do YOU think Micah and his friends should do first to catch this thief?**

▷ **How can YOU be a great friend to someone else in their time of need?**

CHAPTER TWO

Armin looked around the dressing room. All the boys were staring at one another, not sure what to say.

"Come on," said Armin. "We all know it had to have been Chet."

Micah nodded. It did make sense. "We know he was hanging around here after school, since he herded the kindergartners for Miss Petunia. And who knows what he was up to while the rest of us were all busy practicing for the play?"

"Let's not jump to any conclusions," Frank said. "We only know he was at school around the same time the crime was committed. We have no idea if he ever came backstage to the dressing rooms."

"But who else could it be?" Armin asked.

"Hanz is a possibility," Micah said. "He'd totally do something like this."

"Hey!" said Hanz, pulling on his shoes. "Did you forget zat I am standing right here?"

PB was still hunting through his bag, double-checking to make sure nothing was missing. "Micah, it's not very nice to say Hanz would be mean to Armin."

"I am not offended zat you zought I'd be so mean," said Hanz. "I'm offended zat you zought I'd be so boring. Where is ze style in stealing a sketchbook?"

All the boys looked at Hanz in confusion.

"If I vanted to be mean to Armin, I vould do somezing amazing, like skywriting 'Armin is lame' from my jet pack. Or I'd put chemicals in his milk zat turns his skin blue. Or better yet, make his hair rainbow-colored, like ze tail of a stuffed unicorn!" Hanz glanced around. "Somebody should be writing zis stuff down. We don't vant to lose zese great ideas!"

Armin is LAME!

All the other boys looked at each other in confused silence for a few moments.

Finally, Gabe spoke up. "Are you sure you didn't just lose your sketchbook, Armin? I'm always losing stuff. In the last week alone, I've lost my sister's retainer, a ninja mask, two hoagie buns, a sweater vest for my pet possum, my pet possum, three blonde wigs, and a sock—which was particularly weird, since I was wearing it at the time. By the way, has anybody seen my gummy worm costume?"

"You're holding it!" Micah said.

Gabe raised his hands. "Oh. There it is."

"No offense, Gabe," Armin said, "but everyone doesn't lose things quite as easily as you do."

"Then maybe I lost your sketchbook," suggested Gabe.

"That doesn't make sense. You never had my sketchbook."

"Oh yeah."

"Zis has all been very interesting," Hanz sniffed, "but I have to get home. Our amazing French chef is preparing one of his delicacies for dinner. You haven't had chicken fingers until you've had Pierre's chicken fingers!"

"Sorry, Armin," Frank said, "but I have to get out of here too."

The room cleared out, until only Armin and Micah were left.

"I'm sorry, Armin," Micah said. "But don't worry. We'll catch whoever did this. They won't get away with it."

"I still think it was Chet. But why couldn't he have just stolen my math notebook instead?" Armin asked. "There was nothing in there my mom wanted to hang on her wall."

"I don't know about that," Micah said. "The way you multiply fractions is practically a work of art!"

Armin didn't even smile.

Micah used a spoon to break through the gross skin that had congealed on top of the gravy, so he could scoop out the liquid underneath. The skin was usually his favorite thing about having mashed potatoes and gravy, but tonight he just wasn't in the mood.

"Why so glum, Micah?" his dad asked. Only his dad would use a word like "glum." But at least his weird words were better than his dad jokes.

"Which reminds me of a joke . . . ," his dad started. "A horse walked into a restaurant. The waiter looked at him and asked, 'Why the long face?'"

Micah waited for the punch line. Nothing.

"That's the whole joke," his dad said. "When somebody's sad, you ask, 'Why the long face?' But horses always have long faces, see?"

Micah's mom moved the conversation along. "So, what's wrong, Micah?"

Micah sighed. "Armin's sketchbook was stolen out of our dressing room today after school. He's really bummed. He'd spent a ton of time on some of the pictures."

"That's awful!" Micah's dad said. "He's a really talented artist. He showed me a picture of a train he drew that was so lifelike, I could've sworn I heard it whistle."

Micah's mom nodded. "I saw a picture of a vase he drew that was so shiny, I fixed my hair in its reflection!"

"And his painting of the kittens playing gaga ball was absolutely brilliant," said his sister, Audrey.

Everyone stared at her, shocked.

"Are you actually respecting something one of my friends did?" Micah asked, finally.

Audrey shrugged. "I'm as surprised as you are."

Micah's mom passed him the meatloaf, and he cut a slice and slathered it with gravy. He took a half-hearted bite. "Armin thinks it was probably Chet. He was there at school at the time, doing who knows what after detention."

"Just don't forget," Micah's dad said, "innocent until proven guilty. You can't assume someone did something wrong just because they've done something bad to you in the past. You have to have evidence they did this crime."

"But it's not just one thing with Chet. He's always doing bad stuff."

"Still," his mom said, "you have to look at everything separately. Like your dad says, it's not fair to judge somebody without evidence."

"Otherwise, you'll probably be betting on the wrong horse. And then you'll both have long faces." His dad smiled. "You know . . . like a horse. With a long face."

Micah forced a smile. His dad wasn't wrong. About Chet, that is. But that just meant it was time to start gathering evidence.

Actually, now that he thought about it, this

could be fun! He could talk about the case on his vlog, letting his fans know how the investigation was going. He'd probably even get some new fans that way. He'd been stuck on thirteen vlog followers for months. Maybe he'd finally be able to break twenty!

When it was corn dog day in the lunchroom, usually the conversations revolved around what, exactly, the hot dog meat was made of. Chipmunk? Salamander? Old tractor tires? But today the theft in the auditorium dressing room was the topic of the day. There was a flurry of activity around Armin's table, as friends and strangers came up to him to express their condolences or offer their crime-solving tips and theories. Everyone in the school respected Armin's talent in art, so they were taking it more seriously than they would the typical missing lunch box, water bottle, or hoodie.

To Micah's surprise, even Mr. Turtell visited their table for a word. "I don't like that this happened, Armin. I don't like it one bit." He sighed. "I was worried crime would start to escalate once we started to go soft on our rules."

"What rules are you talking about, Mr. Turtell?" Lydia asked.

Mr. Turtell shook his head angrily. "Mrs. Engle's second graders aren't all using safety scissors! Can you believe that? And I actually noticed students in Mr. Martinez's class using #3 pencils! If we can't all use #2 pencils, like civilized people, what other rules will we ignore? Soon it will be anarchy!"

Without waiting for a response, Mr. Turtell shuffled off, shaking his head and mumbling to himself something about slippery slopes.

"Wow," said Lydia. "It doesn't get any weirder than that."

But they didn't have long to mull it over. Something big was going down. Tina Abramowitz and Sebastian Ortiz had just entered through the doors on the far side of the lunchroom.

Tina and Sebastian never came into the lunchroom. Not even on corn dog day.

The reason was, they had special permission to eat in Mrs. Huang's music room so that their band could practice during lunchtime. Philosophical Haircut was the hottest band in all of New Leaf Elementary. (Sure, Rabbit Habit played more gigs on the birthday party circuit—mostly because their music was accessible to moms—but when it came to the "cool" factor, they couldn't compete.)

Tina was the drummer and lead vocalist, while Sebastian played the recorder, triangle, and xylophone. Their brand was mostly emo funk, and all their lyrics were haikus. They weren't just trying to play pop songs you could dance to—no, they were a band that made fifth graders really feel something. Even Lydia respected their talent and passion, even though everyone knew she was more into the

A hush followed the duo as they walked with purpose across the lunchroom, until they finally stopped right in front of Armin.

"Hey Tina. Hey Sebastian," Armin said.

"Hey Armin," Tina responded.

Sebastian said nothing. This didn't surprise Micah. Tina was the talker, while Sebastian was the silent-genius type.

"Normally I'd catch up with you in gym class, but this couldn't wait," Tina said. "We were laying down some sick tracks in the music room when something caught my eye. It was small and floated like a feather in front of the heater vent. I couldn't tell what it was at first, but then I flipped it over and knew right away."

Tina held up a strip of paper that was no bigger than a gum wrapper. She went on. "I couldn't make out the whole picture, but I know you drew it. I'd recognize your delicate pencil lines anywhere."

She handed it to Armin. Micah looked at it over his shoulder. Sure enough, it was a torn piece of paper with a part of one of Armin's drawings on it—it looked like an eye and half a nose from a self-portrait.

"If you ask me," said Tina, "somebody's trying to send a message."

"But what's the message?" asked Micah, utterly confused.

Tina shrugged. "I have no idea. But we can't ignore it. This is too big. It's a crime against art!"

Armin just stared at it, shaking his head sadly. "Thanks, Tina. I appreciate it."

"You're welcome. We artists have to stick together. It's us against the world." Then she and Sebastian turned and walked away, back to the music room.

"Huh," said Lydia. "It turns out, things can always get weirder."

Don't Jump!

Armin assumes Chet stole his sketchbook, but tonight my dad warned me not to jump to conclusions. He's probably right, as usual. Despite his bad jokes, my dad is actually pretty cool.

We need to be smart about this and pay careful attention to the evidence. Even though Chet is a bully, that doesn't automatically make him a thief. It's not fair to assume the worst about someone . . . especially before you can prove it.

That's not easy with guys like Chet. But I guess slowing down and thinking things through is better than just making up crazy ideas about what could have happened. Ugh! This detective work is hard!

Intelligent people are always ready to learn. Their ears are open for knowledge.
Proverbs 18:15 (NLT)

▷ **Have YOU ever been accused of something you didn't do?**

▷ **What can Micah and his friends do next to find out the truth?**

CHAPTER THREE

When Micah told Lydia and Armin what his dad had said about needing hard evidence before coming to any conclusions about who committed the crime, Lydia was on board right away. Micah himself wasn't so sure at first—he still thought jumping to conclusions would save time. But Lydia was probably right, as usual. After all, if they wanted to convince the principal of what happened, finding evidence was a good way to go. Armin went along with it, but figured it didn't matter much either way, since surely any evidence they found would just point to Chet.

They decided the first thing they should do was investigate the crime scene. But it wouldn't be easy. The dressing room wasn't open before school or in the evening. But there was a spare half hour between the end of the school day and the beginning of play rehearsal.

As soon as the final bell of the day rang, Micah shoved his backpack into his locker and rushed to the auditorium, weaving in and out of roughhousing first graders and short-legged kindergartners.

He ran through the empty auditorium to the boys' dressing room in the back. Somehow, by the time he arrived, Lydia and Armin were already there.

"What took you so long?" Armin asked. "Did you stop for a nap?"

Micah ignored him. "Find anything yet?"

The room didn't have a lot going on—it was mostly just an empty space for changing, other than a handful of chairs and a single table pushed into a corner. There were a few hooks and a bulletin board on the walls, but other than that, nothing much to see.

Armin was on his hands and knees, looking under chairs and behind the table. He had brought a magnifying glass from home, and was peering through it at the dust bunnies in every corner. Micah joined him on the ground, his face inches from the floor as he looked closely at the gold-and-blue weave of the carpet.

"What, exactly, are you two looking for?" Lydia asked.

Micah thought about it for a few seconds. "Fingerprints?"

Lydia squinted at him. "In the carpet?"

"Um . . ."

"Well, what did you have in mind, Lydia?" Armin asked.

"I thought maybe we could look around the room and try to figure out all the ways in and out. You know, plot the path of the criminal. See if we could figure out how he snuck in and how he escaped."

Armin and Micah both nodded. "Yeah, I guess that makes more sense."

"So, there's the door we came in through . . . ," said Lydia.

"And this one over here," Micah added, walking across the room and opening a door. He looked inside. "But it's just an empty closet."

Armin walked over to where Micah was. "But there's a window in the closet. That's weird, don't you think?"

Lydia investigated the window. "It's got bars on the outside. I don't think anyone's getting in or out through there, unless they're as skinny as a water noodle."

"Or a gummy worm!" Gabe said proudly as he walked in the room, already in costume. Lucky for him, his mom had cut a hold for his head.

"I don't think a Gabe-sized gummy worm is getting through there," Lydia said.

Gabe opened up the window and pushed his right arm between two of the bars. He nodded. "Lydia was right. I'm stuck."

"Thanks, Gabe," Lydia said dryly. "Very helpful."

Lydia explored the rest of the room while Armin and Micah yanked Gabe's arm out. "The only other way to get in or out of this room is through those two vents—the one in the ceiling and the one in the wall. But both are way too small to even get your head in."

Armin glared at Gabe. "Don't even try it."

Micah sat down on one of the chairs. "So, if I'm understanding this right, there's no way in or out of this room unless you go through the auditorium."

Lydia nodded and sat down beside Micah. "And

nobody saw Chet come in or out of the auditorium after he scootered away."

"Sorry, Armin," Micah said. "It looks like this mystery won't be so easy to solve."

"But Chet is always . . ." Armin started to protest. But then he sighed. "You may be right. It would be hard for him, of all people, to have walked right through the auditorium without anybody noticing. He's huge and not easy to miss."

Armin leaned against the wall. "So, what do we do next?"

"Based on all the cop shows and cartoon mysteries I watch on TV—" Micah started.

"Which are all, I'm sure, extremely realistic," Lydia cut in.

Micah ignored her and finished his sentence: "—we're supposed to figure out who had the motive and opportunity."

Lydia looked at Micah and nodded. "That actually sounds accurate."

"See? You can learn something from TV!"

"Okay." Armin bobbed his head. "Let's start with motive."

"Yeah," said Micah. "We've got to figure out the 'why.' Why would anyone want to steal Armin's art?"

Gabe looked surprised. "Why would anyone not want to steal Armin's art? It's amazing!"

"Great point, Gabe!" Armin said.

Gabe nodded proudly. "Of course! How could we have missed it? It was obviously some famous international art thief who steals Picassos and Monets and Rembrandts! And now Armins!"

"That seems unlikely," said Lydia. "No offense, Armin."

Armin shrugged. "Oh well. A boy can dream."

"I think we're left with only two options," said Micah. "Either someone's out to get Armin, or Tina was right—it's a crime against art."

"Why would anyone have anything against art?" Gabe asked.

"Yeah, that seems unlikely too," Micah agreed. "At least among fifth graders. Everybody I know loves art. That's why they all draw all over the covers of their notebooks when they're supposed to be listening in class."

"So that just leaves us with one option," Lydia said. "We have to think through a list of your enemies, Armin."

"Well, we've already talked about Chet. And there's Hanz, of course. But he . . . somehow actually convinced me that a crime this boring is beneath him."

"Yeah, me too," Micah admitted. "He's just arrogant enough to make that believable."

"I just can't think of anyone else," Armin added.

They sat in silence for a while, thinking things through. Nobody had any answers. Micah watched the dust bunnies hopping around the outside of the vents. Then he watched Lydia grab one of them and hold it up in front of her face.

"If only dust bunnies could talk," she said, shaking her head. "Crime rates would plummet!"

They didn't have any answers, but they weren't ready to give up. After all, there was one other room the criminal must have visited. The music room.

Play rehearsal would start in ten minutes, so they hurried there as fast as they could. They had to go all the way through the auditorium and then backtrack down a hallway just to the right of the auditorium's doors. The music room was at the end of the hall, on the left, and had a large door to accommodate really big instruments, such as tubas, cellos, bass drums, even pianos. The room had several levels so that the music teacher could be in the middle on the lower level with three higher levels surrounding her, all of them able to see everything she was doing. It was sort of like its own mini auditorium.

The left side of the room was filled floor to ceiling with lockers—but they were much, much bigger than ordinary lockers. They had to be big enough to hold tubas, cellos, and bass drums. But not pianos. Nobody steals pianos.

"This room really only has one entrance too," Micah said. "Just the door we came through."

Suddenly the door opened behind them. "What are you kids doing in here?"

It was Dennis, the janitor.

"We're solving a crime!" Gabe said.

"A crime?" Dennis asked. "What kind of crime?"

"Someone stole my sketchbook," Armin said. "And then they ripped up the pages."

"Theft!?! And destruction of property?!?" Dennis shook his head in frustration. "Dadburn hooligans are everywhere. We can't let them get away with this!"

"We're trying not to, sir," Lydia said. "We want to catch the thief."

Dennis kept talking as if he hadn't heard what Lydia said. "Is nothing sacred? Will the lousy, sneaky thieves start stealing teachers' stuff too? Well, not on my watch!"

"That's what we're trying to avoid." Micah said. Dennis still wasn't listening.

Suddenly, the janitor's face went from angry to scared. "Wait! What if they come for the stuff in the janitor's closet! My delicious pastrami sandwiches! The mop I got from my aunt Velma! My box of students' confiscated items."

"Complicated items?" Gabe whispered to Lydia. "Does he mean stuff like mechanical pencils? I can never figure those things out."

"'Confiscated,'" Lydia whispered to Gabe. "Not 'complicated.' It means stuff students weren't supposed to have that their teachers took away from them."

"Oh." Gabe said, still confused.

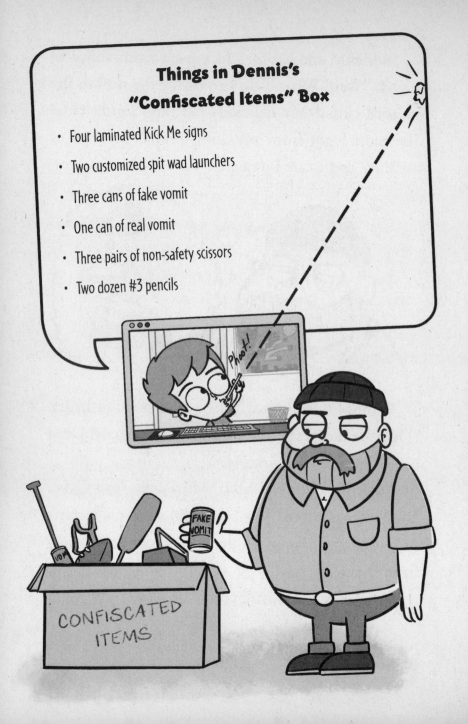

"Sorry. Gotta run," Dennis said as he rushed out the door. "I need to double-check the security system in the janitor's closet. Carry on! I'm rooting for you!"

They could hear his list continue as he hurried down the hall. "My favorite pair of needle-nose pliers! My rat traps! My kitten poster that reminds me not to sweat the small stuff!"

The four friends looked at one another in confused silence.

"Where were we?" Micah finally asked.

"We were examining ways to get in and out of this room," said Lydia.

Armin pointed up at the ceiling. "There's the skylight up there, but it doesn't open. And even if it did, it would be almost impossible to get in and out that way."

"Unless you're a ninja," Gabe said.

Lydia crossed her arms and frowned. "I haven't seen a lot of ninjas skulking around Middletown."

"You wouldn't," Gabe said.

Micah nodded. It was hard to argue with Gabe's logic. Still, they should probably consider other possibilities. He walked to the far wall, behind where the music teacher would lead the orchestra. "There's a vent over here. Where do you think it leads?"

"Who cares?" Armin said. "Just like in the dressing room, the vents are way too small for a person to get through."

Micah looked into the vent. Just like in the

dressing room, there were dust bunnies galore. But there were also some other things in there. But what were they? They looked like thin strips of paper, and he carefully pulled them out.

"Armin, do these pictures look familiar?" Micah held them up.

"It's from one of my self-portraits! That's my ear! And the other one's my chin!"

"Somebody really hates you, Armin," Gabe said.

Micah shrugged. "Or they were just trying to destroy the evidence."

Lydia nodded. "Micah has a good point. We still don't have enough clues to determine the motive yet."

Armin came over to look in the vent for himself. "What's on the other side of this wall, anyway?"

Micah had never thought about it before, but suddenly he could picture the way the rooms of the school were arranged. "This hall follows the length of the auditorium, right?"

"Right," said Lydia.

"So, if this is the last room on the left down this hall, it would be right next to whatever is behind the auditorium on the right."

"The boys' dressing room!" Armin shouted.

"Which means," Lydia said, "these vents are connected. So, if someone shoved scraps of the sketchbook into the dressing room vent, some of them could come through the music room vent!"

"Which means the thief never even had to leave the dressing room for these scraps to end up here!" Armin said.

Armin, Micah, and Lydia looked at each other and nodded. Micah said first what they were all thinking: "Everything seems to be pointing to the fact that it was someone who had access to the boys' dressing room, which means it was someone in the play."

Armin shook his head in anger. "In other words, it was an inside job!"

Guilty as Charged

Dennis got pretty worked up about the idea that there was a thief in the school! He can be a bit unusual sometimes, but he's not wrong about how serious this is. Sure, I mess up now and then, but I would never steal anything!

Well . . . except that time I ate one of Audrey's cupcakes she'd gotten from a birthday party (I blamed the dog). And . . . oh yeah. There was that time I took some quarters from the change tray in my dad's car without asking, for the vending machine at school. And, of course, there's all the days I steal more time for video games even though my mom wants me to stop after an hour.

Wow! I guess I'm a thief too! I need to remember that even stealing "small" things is not right. I'm so glad God forgives us when we ask Him to!

Do not steal or tell lies or cheat others. Leviticus 19:11 (CEV)

▷ **Have YOU ever taken something that didn't belong to you?**

▷ **What should Micah (and YOU) do to make it right?**

CHAPTER FOUR

Micah, Lydia, Armin, and Gabe knew what they needed to do next. Well, Micah, Lydia, and Armin knew what they needed to do next. Gabe was just along for the ride.

Once again, Micah leaned heavily on what he'd learned from cop shows and cartoon mysteries. According to TV's best detectives, the next step was to interview the suspects. Break them down. Put the pressure on. Get them in a room, crank up the heat, and question them until they broke.

Miss Petunia was letting Micah, Lydia, and Armin out of rehearsal for the day to carry out this part of the investigation. When she'd found out a crime against art had been committed, she was on board with doing whatever it took to solve it. She was more than happy to throw all the resources of the drama department on the case. Which mostly came down to letting Micah, Lydia, and Armin out of rehearsal and giving them permission to question the rest of the cast of *Don't You Carrot All?* one by one.

Unfortunately, New Leaf didn't come equipped with an interrogation room. The principal's office seemed like the obvious choice, with its general air of justice and intimidation, but Mr. Drury refused to let them take over his space. For some reason he didn't think it was smart to loan out his office to three elementary school kids so they could interrogate students about a missing sketchbook that may or may not have been stolen. Go figure.

Dennis, on the other hand, was 100 percent on board with them using the janitor's office. And it was absolutely perfect! Weird, but perfect.

Micah, Armin, Gabe, and Lydia all gathered outside Dennis's office on Wednesday after school, and he ushered them in.

"I can't stay," he told them. "I have to go fix Miss Termudgeon's pencil sharpener. What part of 'pencil sharpener' don't kindergartners understand? You can't use them to sharpen pens, paintbrushes, Twizzlers, or Katie Lubnick's hair.

"Anyway, I'm going to let you kids stay here without me." He stared at them each in turn and nodded at an enormous safe in the corner. "I lock up all my valuables now anyway, since the crime wave started. No one's getting my sandwiches!"

Don't worry," said Armin. "We'd never take your sandwiches."

"We're on the side of justice!" Gabe chimed in.

"So am I!" Dennis said. "And I want that sneaky thief caught, so I'll help you any way I can."

With those words of confidence, Dennis left. The kids looked around. He wasn't wrong—there wasn't much to steal. Other than the safe in the corner (which, in addition to holding Dennis's sandwiches, probably held his most valuable tools), there were a couple of shelves with some buckets, paintbrushes, and other odds and ends. A few brooms and mops stood in a corner, and two things were hanging on the wall: the kitten poster Dennis had mentioned before, and a Garfield calendar. Gabe stepped up to the calendar and starting flipping through the comics.

The Garfield jokes made Gabe laugh so hard he peed a little. His friends kindly pretended they didn't notice him trying to cover up the wet spot on his pants.

What's on Dennis's Calendar for Today?

8:00   Fix a hole in the heating duct

9:30   Clean animal poop out of the heating duct

11:00   Clean up after the latest fire in Mr. Beaker's lab. Remind
        Mr. Beaker not to do experiments using cafeteria food, as it is
        highly flammable

1:00   After recess, rescue kickballs stuck in trees

1:05   After recess, rescue kindergartners stuck in trees

1:30   Buy a safe so kids don't steal my tools, sandwiches, confiscated
        items, etc.

2:30   Fix the filter in Miss Tinker's aquarium so fish stop dying

3:30   Unclog the toilet near Miss Tinker's class from all the flushed fish

4:00   Let three kids into my office to solve a crime

The only other thing in the room was a small table in the middle with a few chairs around it and a light overhead.

Micah smiled. "This will be perfect for our interrogations!"

"Can I go first?" Gabe asked.

"You mean you want to ask the first question?" Armin asked him.

"No, I want to be interrogated!"

Lydia squinted at him. "Do you even know what 'interrogated' means?"

Gabe grinned, thrilled to be asked a question he knew the answer to. "Of course I do! It's what farmers do to their crops when they spray them with water to help them grow."

"Actually, you're thinking of 'irrigated,'" said Lydia. "'Interrogated,' on the other hand, means we'll ask you a bunch of really tough questions so we can figure out if you're guilty or innocent."

"Even better!" said Gabe. "It's like a game show!"

"Kind of, I guess," Micah said.

Gabe sat down at the table. "Let me have it!"

Micah shrugged. "Okay then. Where were you on the afternoon of Monday the 26th?"

Gabe crossed his arms, doing his best 'tough guy' look. "That depends."

"On?" Armin asked.

"What day is it now?"

"Wednesday the 28th," Lydia answered.

"Oh. So how many days ago was that?"

"Two," said Armin, Micah, and Lydia, all at the same time.

A surprised look came over Gabe's face. "Hey Armin! Wasn't that the day your sketchbook was stolen?"

"Gabe!" Lydia snapped. "Do you even know what we're doing here?"

"Um . . ." Gabe looked around. "I think it had something to do with a pencil sharpener. Or maybe a sandwich."

Micah sighed. "We're here to investigate who

stole Armin's sketchbook. And for some reason you volunteered to be the first one questioned. So, we're asking you: what were you doing on the afternoon it was stolen?"

Gabe sat back, getting comfortable. "Well, it all started with me getting into costume, taking on the role of a gummy worm in Miss Petunia's play. I slipped the big, red sleeping bag over my head and pushed my arms and legs through the holes. Sadly, no one remembered to cut a hole for my head, so I was flying blind. But when I thought about it, I realized gummy worms don't have eyes either, so this would be a great way to get into character!"

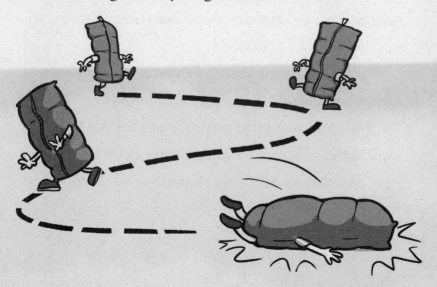

Armin motioned for Gabe to move the story along more quickly. "And what was the first thing you did after getting in costume?"

"I wriggled on my belly until I fell down the steps! It was awesome! Just like a real gummy worm would do."

Lydia looked at Micah and Armin and shook her head in confusion. "I have so many questions."

"Unfortunately," Armin said, "we've got to keep this moving."

Gabe went on. "Then I thought to myself, what would a gummy worm do next? He'd crawl around in the dirt! I had to find the dirtiest place near the auditorium, so I went into the boys' dressing room."

"Good call," Lydia said.

"Yeah!" Gabe nodded. "I don't think anyone's vacuumed that room in years! After crawling around for a while, I unzipped part of the sleeping bag and looked out. There were dust bunnies everywhere!"

"Did you see anything suspicious while you were in there?" Micah asked.

"No, me and Ronnie didn't see much."

"Ronnie?" Armin asked. "Who's Ronnie?"

"I named the dust bunnies. Ronnie was the biggest. We're friends now. He's here in my sock if you want to irrigate him too."

"Interrogate," said Lydia.

"Tomato, potato."

Armin sighed. "Do you remember seeing my sketchbook while you were in there?"

"Nope. It wasn't there anymore. I remember when you got dressed in your costume, you put it on the bench in the corner by the heating duct. I remember because the breeze from the heater was making the corners of the pages move. But then when Ronnie and I were in there crawling around later, it was nowhere to be seen."

"And you never saw anyone else come or go from the room?"

"I didn't see anyone, but I did hear something when I first went in."

"What did you hear?" Armin asked.

"Somebody shuffling around in the corner. They must've been really quick, because by the time I got the sleeping bag unzipped, they were nowhere to be seen."

"And you didn't hear them run out the door?"

"Nope! They must have been quick and quiet. I still think we need to revisit my ninja theory."

Lydia puffed out her cheeks in exasperation. "Okay, we'll consider that," she said. "But in the meantime, do you remember when you went into the dressing room? Or what time you heard the person run out the door?"

"It was right away after Miss Petunia's speech. Right at the beginning of rehearsal."

Micah nodded. At least now they'd be able to put a timeline together. "Is there anything else you want to tell us? Anything at all?"

"Nope. Fell down the stairs. Made friends with a dust bunny. Heard a ninja. I think that covers it."

"Okay, then," said Armin with a sigh. "I guess you're free to go."

"So, when does the farmer come and water me?"

Lydia shook her head. "Again, you're thinking of 'irrigation.' This was an 'interrogation.'"

"Oh yeah."

Gabe looked so disappointed, Micah had to end things on a hopeful note. "But maybe next time."

The kids decided Chet should be next in line for questioning. Even though Micah and Lydia didn't think he'd committed the crime (although Armin still had his suspicions), they thought it would be a good idea to at least find out if he'd seen anything fishy while he was on the school grounds.

Chet was easy to find. He always spent the first hour after school in detention, and Dennis volunteered to go bring him to the janitor's office. Mr. Turtell was the detention teacher, and all Dennis had to do was tell him he needed to bring Chet in for questioning. Mr. Turtell assumed Chet had broken something or spilled something or caused some other kind of mess somewhere. You know: the usual.

"So, dorks, what am I doing here?" Chet asked as he strutted into the janitor's room.

Micah motioned to the table, and Chet had a seat. Micah and Lydia sat beside him while Armin stayed standing.

"Someone stole Armin's sketchbook," Lydia answered.

"I didn't do it!" Chet shouted.

"We don't think you did." Micah spoke in the soothing voice he used whenever he was calming down angry bullies. This was not his first time.

"Micah's right," Lydia said. "It was stolen in the dressing room behind the auditorium, and there's no way in or out of there except from backstage. After you left, we don't think there would have been any way for you to sneak back in and steal it."

"Then like I asked before, nerds, what am I doing here?"

"We'd like you to answer a few questions about anything you may have seen after school that day," Armin answered. "Maybe it will help us solve the puzzle."

"And why should I help you?"

Micah fielded this one. "Because maybe if you help us solve this crime, the authorities will go easier on you next time they catch you for something." Micah had no idea if this was true, but it was worth a shot.

Chet nodded. "I can get behind that."

"So," Lydia started. "Where did you go after you herded the kindergartners and left the auditorium?"

"I went out to the playground. Kids like to swing and play four square when they're in after-school care."

"And what did you do there?"

"Just normal, everyday bullying."

"Bullying?" Armin asked. "Could you be more specific?"

"You know," said Chet, "giving wedgies, shooting water balloons at kids, stealing lunch money. The usual."

"Who did you bully?" Micah asked. He was surprised Chet was being so open about this. Maybe if they couldn't nail him for the theft of the sketchbook, they could put him away on bullying charges. Or at least that's what they'd do on the cop shows and cartoon mysteries he watched.

"Just some other kids on the playground," said Chet. He suddenly looked a little nervous. "You know the type. Mostly small and puny. Nerds and dorks like you."

Micah stared at Lydia. A strange look had come over her face. Like she had a new theory. "Just give us a name or two. So they can back up your story."

"Uh . . . uh . . . ," Chet stammered. "Nerds and dorks all kind of blend together to me. I don't really know any of their names."

"Could you pick any of them out of the yearbook?"

"I . . . maybe," Chet said. Under the bright light, Micah could see he was really sweating now.

Lydia didn't let up. Micah was impressed—she was relentless! "And after you picked them out of the yearbook, if we asked them to back up your story, they'd agree you were there bullying them?"

"Um . . . probably not," Chet confessed. "Dorks

and nerds have terrible memories. It's embarrassing, really. I mean, like, sometimes I'll give the same kid a wedgie for weeks and he still forgets my name!"

Lydia twisted the desk lamp around so it was shining in Chet's face, then stared him in the eye. "You're hiding something!"

"What? Why would I . . . What do I have to hide? I'm a bully! Everybody knows it."

Micah was starting to get suspicious too. "Something's not adding up here. What aren't you telling us?"

"Nothing! I swear I didn't take the sketchbook. Please, just drop it."

Armin slammed his hand on the table. "We'll drop it if you tell us the truth about what you were doing after you left the auditorium!"

"Yeah!" Micah joined in. "We want to know what's really going on!"

"Tell us!" Lydia shouted.

Suddenly, a look came over Chet's face that Micah had never expected—a look of defeat.

"Fine! You win!" he shouted. "It's true. I wasn't really bullying! I was"—he swallowed hard, like he was having trouble getting his next word out—"reading. There, I said it. It's true. Sometimes I like to read."

Lydia, Armin, and Micah gasped in surprise. Not in a million years would they have expected this. Everyone just sat there, trying to take it all in.

Finally, Micah broke the silence. "So . . . what were you reading?"

He expected the answer would be a comic book.

That was the obvious choice, right? Or maybe a sports magazine. Even a book about dinosaurs or man-eating carnivores would have made sense. But he never saw coming what actually came out of Chet's mouth next.

Chet took a deep breath. "*For the Love of a Dolphin*, book 2 in the Dolphin Heart series. I can't get enough of them! Nothing will ever come between Tessa and Shasta, her dolphin friend! My heart melts just thinking about their bond!"

"Um . . . ," Micah faltered. He looked at Armin and Lydia. Their mouths were wide-open in shock. No one knew what to say.

"I believe you," Armin finally said. Micah and Lydia nodded.

"Good," said Chet. "But if you tell anyone else, I'll flatten all three of you."

Lydia shrugged. "And just like that, things are back to normal."

A Lightbulb Moment

What a weird day! Who knew Chet had a soft spot for dolphin books? I guess he could be making it all up, but I don't think he's that good of an actor. Besides, he wouldn't ruin his reputation as a bully just to get out of trouble. He loves getting in trouble!

It's surprising to see Chet in a whole new light. It makes me wonder: what does God think about Chet? The Bible says God loves everyone. It's hard to understand that. There are so many people in the world, and a lot of them are just plain mean!

God must be looking at things the rest of us just can't see. And I guess that's great news for all of us.

For God so loved the world, that he gave his only Son, that whoever believes in him should not perish but have eternal life. John 3:16 (ESV)

▷ **Are there people in your life who are hard to love?**

▷ **What could YOU do to see them the way God does?**

CHAPTER FIVE

After Chet's interrogation, the kids questioned the cast of *Don't You Carrot All?* one by one. Compared to Gabe and Chet, the rest of the interviews were normal-ish. That's as good as you can expect when you're talking to kids like Hanz, PB and J, and the kindergarten vegetable soup crew. Even though they tried to keep the questioning down to a few minutes apiece, it took all of rehearsal to get through them, and they were exhausted by the end.

Lydia talked Micah and Armin into coming to school early the next day so they could debrief about the interrogations. They met in the auditorium, threw their bags in a corner, then sat in the cushioned seats. The first thing on Micah's agenda was to ask Lydia what "debrief" meant. It turned out it had nothing to do with underpants. It basically just meant she wanted to talk about what happened in the interrogations and see if they were any closer to solving the case.

"So," Lydia began, "who don't we trust?"

"Chet. Hanz. PB and J," said Micah.

Lydia sighed. "I don't mean who don't we trust in general. I mean who don't we trust when it comes to the stolen sketchbook."

"Yeah, that make more sense."

Armin shrugged. "That's a tough one. Everyone had a pretty good story. I totally believe Chet now. There's no way he'd make up that story about reading. It's just too humiliating."

"And I know Gabe didn't do it," Micah said. "He's weird, but honest. I can't imagine him stealing anything, especially from his friends."

Lydia nodded. "And everyone else had an alibi during the time the crime was committed at the very beginning of rehearsal."

"What's an alibi?" Gabe asked. "I want one too!"

"An alibi," Lydia huffed, "is when someone else vouches for you, saying you were with them, so you couldn't have committed the crime. The kindergartners were with each other. Frank and PB and J have most of their scenes together, so they didn't have a chance to sneak off by themselves."

"Most of Hanz's scenes are with me, unfortunately," Micah said. "And anyway, like I said before, I tend to believe him when he tells us he wouldn't do something as boring to Armin as stealing his notebook. He usually does get a little fancier with his crimes."

"So where does that leave us?" Armin said with a sigh.

"Almost late for class," Lydia answered, looking at her watch.

Without any new ideas, or even a decent new

theory they could chew on, they got up to get their school stuff out of the corner where they'd tossed it. But as Micah walked up to the pile of coats, backpacks, and lunchboxes, something looked wrong.

"Did we really leave everything scattered all over like this?" Micah asked.

"Yeah, it's a real mess," Armin said. "Almost like someone's been tossing things around while we weren't paying attention."

Lydia scrunched up her face in confusion as she gathered her things. "I didn't hear anyone come in. Did either of you?"

"Nope."

"Nope."

"Hey, my lunch!" Lydia shouted. "Somebody opened it up! And they ate my sandwich!"

"What kind was it?" Micah asked.

"Really?" said Lydia. "That's the first thing you say to me? Someone's been going through my stuff, eating my food, and the first thing you want to know is what kind of sandwich I packed?"

"I just wondered . . . ," Micah said, then started over. "I'm really sorry somebody stole your sandwich, Lydia. Did they take anything else?"

Lydia went through the rest of her lunchbox, her backpack, and even the pockets of her coat. "No, it doesn't look like it." Then she looked up at Micah.

"And it was all-natural peanut butter, by the way."

"So, they just ate the sandwich and nothing else?" Armin asked. "What else did you pack in your lunchbox?"

"Some celery sticks and a cookie."

"Whoa! Who on earth would take a peanut butter sandwich and leave behind a cookie?" Micah asked. "What kind of a cookie was it, anyway?"

"Whole wheat, cranberry, and almond crunch bar."

"Oh," Micah nodded. "That makes more sense."

"Hey!" Lydia snapped.

Armin looked at her and shrugged. "You gotta admit, that hardly even counts as a cookie."

"Whatever."

They gathered the rest of their stuff and headed toward the big auditorium doors. Just as they opened them up and got ready to jump into the rush-hour traffic of kids, Lydia turned to Armin and Micah. She had a half smile on her face. "Well, I guess having my lunch stolen is good news and bad news."

"What's the good news?" Armin asked.

"Well, now that there's a second crime, maybe we'll find some new evidence."

"And the bad news?" Micah asked.

"Now I'm going to have to buy the school lunch. Liver and squash casserole."

Armin wrinkled his nose in distaste. "I'll give you half my sandwich."

"That's nice of you, Armin. And I'll give you half my wheat, cranberry, and almond bar."

"No thanks. I'm good."

Nothing unexpected happened the rest of the school day. Katie Floss swallowed one of Miss Tinker's goldfish, Zach Duke accidentally glued himself to an alphabet chart, Frank Millwood got 125% on his history test (how is that even possible?), and there was another explosion in Mr. Beaker's lab." In other words, it was just another typical day at New Leaf Elementary. (Side note: always wear safety goggles when mixing hydrochloric acid with the cafeteria's liver and squash casserole.)

After school Micah, Lydia, and Armin went to play practice. Whenever they weren't practicing their scenes, they spent their time looking for evidence that the sandwich thief may have left behind. But there was almost nothing to show for their efforts. They only found a half inch of bread crust and a small smudge of all-natural peanut butter on the carpet. Other than that, the criminal disappeared without a trace. It seemed to Micah that this must be the work of a professional. Lydia gathered the bread crust and peanut butter smudge in a ziplock bag, then wrote "evidence" on the bag in permanent marker. Maybe the police could use it to help build their case.

Micah was excited to get home after practice. Thursday night, right after dinner, was when his family all gathered in the living room to watch a TV show. And not just any show, the very greatest show on television. *Maxx Dryver: Officer of Justice.* And even better, last week's episode had ended on a cliffhanger! Would Maxx escape from Vladimir Typhoon and his evil henchmen? Micah had been wondering all week.

Maxx Dryver was by far the greatest character anyone had ever created in the entire history of the world. He was smart. He was strong. He was funny. He even had two *x*'s in his first name!

Everyone in his family loved the show—including Audrey, although she pretended not to. Sure, she made fun of the "corny dialogue" and "hokey endings," but every once in a while, Micah would glance over at her as she watched, and he'd see a look of wonder and excitement on her face. Even a grumpy teenager was no match for Maxx Dryver!

His parents liked the show because it was safe for the whole family, but usually that was code for "boring." But this was a rare exception. If Maxx Dryver didn't get your heart pounding, you might need to check your ticker for glitches.

Boring Shows That Micah's Parents Love

- *Secrets of Sudoku!*
- *The Great Needlepoint Throwdown*
- *Lighthouse Painters in Focus*
- *The Groaners* (the annual dad joke award ceremony)
- *Healthy Home Cooking with Quinoa and Kale*
- *Guess How Much My Old Stuff Is Worth!*
- *Masterpiece Theatre Presents: Anything*

By the first ten minutes of the episode, Maxx had gotten out of Vladimir's exploding warehouse trap. Then, with heart-pounding excitement, Maxx snuck around Vlad's facilities, gathering evidence as he tried to avoid henchmen around every corner. (Micah wasn't exactly sure what a henchman was—he figured it was a man who "henched" a lot, whatever that meant—but he knew they meant trouble for Maxx!)

At the end of the episode, Maxx took all the evidence he'd found back to a crime lab. And that's when, to Micah's great surprise, he found himself watching the show in a completely different way! He started hearing words like "DNA evidence" and "forensics" and "criminal profiling." He even found himself listening very carefully to the details of what Maxx had gathered from the crime scenes and how they were testing the evidence.

Micah used to zone out during this stuff as he waited for the next chase scene. Maybe someday he could return to those simpler times. But right now, these details mattered! After all, he had his own crime to solve!

During a commercial break, Micah got up from his seat on the couch and went to the kitchen.

"Where are you going?" his mom asked.

"Looking for a notepad in the junk drawer."

"Why?"

"To take notes."

Audrey shook her head. "I keep thinking you can't get any weirder, but there you go again."

Micah ignored her. When the show came back on, he started writing as fast as he could, jotting down everything Maxx and his cohorts were saying about the science of crime. He even jotted down the words he didn't understand. In fact, he especially jotted down the words he didn't understand. If he was really going to learn about this stuff, he'd need to (slight shudder) increase his vocabulary.

The next morning Micah proudly showed Lydia and Armin his notes.

"Well, what do you think?"

Lydia shrugged. "For starters, 'forensic' doesn't have a *z* in it. And 'toxicology' only makes sense if someone's been poisoned. I don't think anyone's been poisoned by our criminal."

"Unless you count the fact that the criminal forced you to eat liver and squash casserole," said Armin.

Micah sighed. "You're both missing the point! We need a real scientist to help us! Maybe even a laboratory!"

"Where are we going to get those?" Armin asked. "We don't know any crime scene investigators or forensic experts."

"But we do know a real scientist."

Lydia and Armin stared blankly at him.

Micah stared right back, as if they were both dense. "Mr. Beaker, of course!"

"But . . . ," both Lydia and Armin said at the same time.

"It's just that . . . ," Armin started, then concluded, "Mr. Beaker is a little . . . weird."

"Sure, he's a bit clumsy. And his experiments rarely work. And he's almost always accidentally setting something on fire." Micah paused, forgetting where he was going with this.

"But?" Armin asked.

Micah remembered. "But he's really smart! Think of all the big words he knows that we don't know! I bet he even knew that there wasn't a *z* in 'forensic.'"

Lydia snorted. "Yep. That's the sign of a true genius."

Micah sighed. "What other choice do we have? I don't see either of you getting anywhere with this investigation."

"Fine," said Lydia. "But if he tries one experiment with a school lunch, I'm out of there!"

Micah nodded. "That's fair."

Mr. Beaker's lab was just as it always was. On the shelves and desks were test tubes of mysterious liquids, a dozen or so microscopes, and several Bunsen burners for heating up chemicals. The walls were covered with periodic tables, posters of the solar system, and pictures of plant and animal parts. And as usual, the air had that pleasant "recent fire" smell that all the kids at New Leaf Elementary had come to know and love.

Like his lab, Mr. Beaker was just as he always was. He wore his white lab coat, and a pair of safety goggles was perched on top of his head. Puffy tufts of hair sprang out of his temples, and a little sprouted from his ears as well.

"Welcome, welcome," said Mr. Beaker. "I do appreciate you giving up your recess to learn science! I think you may find it even more enjoyable than your usual games of tug and three square."

"Don't you mean 'tag' and 'four square'?" Micah asked.

"Yes, yes. Of course. I was never much for children's games myself. Ever since I was a child, learning was my recess, and experiments were my games!"

"Then we've come to the right place," Lydia said politely. "We need your help."

Mr. Beaker nodded, then stared into the distance at nothing in particular. The kids looked at each other and shrugged.

"Is there something we can help *you* with?" Micah asked.

"I'm sorry," said Mr. Beaker. "I thought I smelled something burning."

The kids all looked around. Nothing seemed on fire at the moment.

"No, it's probably just in the air from earlier," said Lydia.

Mr. Beaker nodded. "I have to be extra vigilant these days! Principal Drury is starting to keep a chart. If there are three more explosions this week, he'll take away my Bunsen burners.

Micah nodded. Seemed fair. "Well, what we're here for shouldn't require lighting anything on fire. We need your help with a crime."

"Do you want to solve one or commit one?" Mr. Beaker asked.

Armin, Micah, and Lydia exchanged glances.

"Solve one, of course," said Lydia.

Mr. Beaker shrugged. "That's probably for the best. Well, give me the details, and tell me what evidence you've collected so far."

Since it was Micah's idea to ask Mr. Beaker for help, he gave him the gist of the story. Lydia and Armin piped up whenever Micah got a detail wrong or left something out. They shared about the missing sketchbook, of course, as well as the investigating and interrogating they'd done so far. They talked about their busted theories, and then how Lydia's sandwich had suddenly gone missing as well— almost right from under their noses. Finally, Micah told him about all he'd learned from Maxx Dryver.

To no one's surprise, Mr. Beaker was unfamiliar with the show—he mostly watched *Nova*, whatever that was. But when Micah described it to him, he applauded Maxx's use of forensic science. As it turned out, "forensic" just meant the science of solving crimes. (Micah realized he probably should have figured this out from "context clues"—another term he'd learned from Maxx Dryver. Now, at least, he didn't have to look it up! Looking things up was the worst.)

After hearing their story, Mr. Beaker looked as excited as Micah had ever seen him. "So, where's the evidence you brought me to investigate?"

Armin dug in his backpack until he found what he was looking for. "Here are the scraps of paper the thief left behind," he said, handing them to the teacher. "You think you could find fingerprints on them?"

Mr. Beaker squinted at the scraps. "Anyone can find fingerprints on glass, or even glossy wood. But paper is notoriously bad at holding fingerprints. Which makes finding them all the more fun!"

If these words had come out of most people's mouths, Micah would have thought they were being sarcastic. But this was truly Mr. Beaker's idea of fun. He went into one of his cabinets, grabbed a small bottle, and held it out for the kids to look at. "This aluminum powder helps fingerprints show up on all sorts of surfaces. Hold one of the paper strips down on the desk, and I'll gently pour some powder over it."

After Mr. Beaker had poured out a small pile of powder, he took a deep breath and blew it off, none too carefully. A cloud of powder filled the air, and Micah, Lydia, and Armin all started coughing. Mr. Beaker didn't notice. He held up the scrap of paper and pulled a magnifying glass out of one of his lab coat pockets.

"There! Can you see that? The aluminum is adhering to the oils in the fingerprints. If you look closely you can see the bumps and ridges of the prints!"

"I can't see it," Armin said, stretching himself over Lydia's shoulder, who was standing right next to Micah, who was beside Mr. Beaker.

Mr. Beaker plugged an overhead projector into a power strip next to the wall. "Let's try this!"

They could now see the whole strip of paper blown up on a screen. Mr. Beaker grinned from ear to ear. "Look at that big fingerprint on the corner! And there's another good one on top! Now we're getting somewhere!"

"And both the prints look exactly the same, so they must have come from the same person," Micah said. "We just need to find that finger!"

Armin was looking closely at his hand. "I think I may be able to find it."

"So it was you!" Micah said. "Why would you tear up your own art?"

Armin glared at him. "I wouldn't! That's ridiculous!"

Lydia shook her head. "Actually, Armin probably just got fingerprints on the paper when he was drawing the picture."

"Oh." Micah nodded. "That makes more sense."

They spent a few moments looking for other prints on the scraps, but none showed up.

"Dead end," Micah declared.

"There's no such thing as dead ends in forensics!" Mr. Beaker said enthusiastically. "Now we test the sandwich crust!"

"You can find fingerprints on a sandwich?" Lydia asked.

"Of course not. Paper is difficult to dust for prints, but Wonder Bread is absolutely impossible! That's why sandwiches are so popular among criminals."

Micah, Armin, and Lydia looked at each other skeptically.

"So how do we test it, then?" Lydia asked.

"Odontology!"

"Olly olly oxen free?" Micah asked.

"Odontology," Mr. Beaker said again. "Teeth marks. We carefully look at the teeth marks and compare them to the dental records of our suspects."

"But how do we get the dental records of our suspects?" Micah asked.

Mr. Beaker shrugged. "Crime lab scientists

usually leave that up to the cops." He looked at the crust under his magnifying glass. "Hmm . . . the thief seems to have a very small mouth. Look at these little bite marks."

Micah nodded. "Do you think it could have been a kindergartner? They still have their baby teeth."

"Could be," Mr. Beaker said.

Next, he put the bread crust on a small glass slide and pulled a microscope over to their desk. He plugged it into the power strip beside the overhead projector, then hunched over the microscope's eyepiece.

"Are you looking for DNA?" Lydia asked.

"Sadly, our microscopes aren't powerful enough for that. I'm just looking to see what else I can find. Wow! This crust is crawling with microbes! Where did you find it?"

"On the floor of the auditorium," Lydia answered.

"Remind me not to use the 'five-second rule' when I drop food in there," Micah said.

Mr. Beaker nodded. "And as for any DNA that might be on the crust, I know a guy who works in a lab at Metro Police headquarters. Maybe he could take a look for us. I'll give him a call."

"Really?" Armin asked. "That would be awesome!"

Mr. Beaker looked at his cell phone. "Drat. Out of battery. Luckily I have my charger with me."

He grabbed it off his desk and walked back over to the power strip.

Something about the number of cords coming out of the strip suddenly made Micah nervous. Hadn't his dad warned him about having too many of his electronics plugged in at the same time?

Micah was thinking about saying something, but Mr. Beaker plugged the charger in right before he got around to it.

Suddenly, there was a bang and a loud crackling sound! The lights dimmed. A spark shot out of the strip. As if in slow motion, Micah watched the spark sail through the air like a tiny fireworks display, until at last it landed on one of the strips of sketchbook paper Armin still held in his hand.

Immediately, the paper caught on fire. Armin

looked down and screamed, then dropped it on the carpet.

Which immediately also caught on fire.

Without even flinching, Mr. Beaker walked over to the wall, grabbed the extinguisher, and sprayed down the flames.

The kids and Mr. Beaker all stared at one another in silence.

"Wow, Mr. Beaker," Micah said at last. "It sure is amazing how fires seem to pop up whenever you're around."

"It's my gift and my curse," Mr. Beaker agreed. "But if you don't mind, could you not mention this one to Mr. Drury?"

God's Amazing Creation

We haven't figured out who stole Armin's sketchbook yet, but we had fun hanging out in Mr. Beaker's lab. Science is amazing! Who knew?

When I really start paying attention to all the stuff God made and how it works, it blows my mind. You can actually look at tiny parts of cells under a microscope and figure out who or what they belong to! That means God took the time to make each one of us unique.

Man, I should start paying more attention in science class. Who knows what I could learn next?

Thank you for making me so wonderfully complex! Psalm 139:14 (NLT)

▷ **What is something God made that YOU find amazing?**

▷ **How can YOU pay more attention to God's wonderful creation?**

CHAPTER SIX

What to do next? That was the question that kept Armin, Micah, and Lydia deep in thought over the weekend. Despite what Mr. Beaker had told them about no dead ends in forensics, it sure felt like they were at one. Lydia wanted to wait until the DNA tests came back, but the others weren't sure what good that would do. After all, they didn't have DNA samples of anyone in the school to compare them to.

Before school on Monday, they gathered in the hallway to talk over the case.

"Well, I think we should do some criminal profiling," Lydia said. "We need to analyze the psychology of a criminal who would want to confiscate a sketchbook and then consume a peanut butter sandwich while curiously leaving a wheat cranberry nut bar behind."

Micah looked at her blankly.

Lydia got the picture. "Which words didn't you understand this time?"

Micah rubbed his chin. "Let's see. 'Psychology,' 'confiscate,' 'analyze,' and 'consume.'"

Lydia sighed. "Forget it!"

Micah was hoping she'd say that. Criminal profiling sounded boring. Score one for having a bad vocabulary!

"I think we should do a stakeout," Micah suggested. "Maxx Dryver does those all the time! All night long he and his partner, Spike Hubbings, secretly spy on crime dens from the back of a van. It sounds awesome! I'll bring the snacks."

Lydia looked exasperated. "Don't you think there may be more important things to figure out than just who's bringing the snacks?"

"Like?" Micah asked.

"Like where are we having the stakeout? Are we spying on someone in particular, or are we setting some kind of trap? What's the plan?"

"Ooh!" Armin said. "I like the trap idea. Let's get some stuff we think the thief would want to steal and plant it somewhere, then spy on it and see what happens."

"That's brilliant!" Micah yelped.

"Not exactly 'brilliant,' but I guess it's a start," Lydia said. "Okay then. What should we use as bait, and where do we put it?"

"Armin, do you have any other artwork you'd be willing to sacrifice?" Micah asked. "Maybe some old paint-by-numbers?"

Armin looked offended. "Excuse me? I don't do paint by numbers!"

"Sorry!" Micah was a little annoyed. Who did Armin think he was? Paint-by-numbers is awesome!

Armin shrugged. "That said, I could probably spare a hand turkey I made in art class."

"And I could spare a peanut butter sandwich," Lydia said. "Although that would mean eating school lunch again. What are they serving?"

"Lima bean egg rolls," Micah said.

Lydia scrunched up her face. "Oh well. I guess we all have to sacrifice."

Suddenly Micah felt Lydia's and Armin's eyes on him.

"Actually, Micah hasn't sacrificed anything yet." said Armin. "For some reason nobody's stolen anything of his."

"How is that my fault?" Micah asked.

"I'm not saying it's your fault. I was just stating a fact."

"Well, stop stating facts!"

"Then what should I state?"

Lydia sighed. "This is the most ridiculous argument I've ever heard. We all want to catch the thief, right? So where are we going to put the trap, and where are we going to watch from?"

"Fine!" said Armin. "I think the trap should be

in the auditorium. That seems to be the center of all the criminal activity."

"That sounds like a good idea," Micah agreed. "We just need to figure out a place to watch from."

"The catwalk!" Lydia shouted.

Armin's eyes grew wide. "Do you mean the flimsy little walkway thirty feet in the air?"

"Yep!" Lydia answered, not seeming to notice his terrified look. "It's where they control all the stage lights. We could stay up there quietly when we're not rehearsing our parts onstage. We can see everything from up there."

"What about the guy who does the lights for the play? Won't he come up there?" Micah asked.

"No one does lights for rehearsals."

Armin shook his head. "I really don't think this is a good idea."

"What, are you scared of heights?" Micah asked.

Armin looked down at his shoes. "Maybe."

Lydia shrugged. "Well, if we want to catch the thief, you'd better get over it. It's the best idea we've had yet." Then she sighed. "And yes, I know that's not saying much."

After school Micah took a quick trip to the Gas & Snacks store on the corner to buy a bagful of snacks, then rushed back to play rehearsal.

Lydia looked at his bag. "Looks like you brought enough snacks for a week."

"You never know," said Micah.

Miss Petunia decided to begin rehearsal by trying to teach the kindergartners their big vegetable soup square dance—onions do-si-doing with carrots, while beets and okra "swing their partners 'round and 'round." That sort of thing. Armin, Lydia, and Micah figured they had at least forty-five minutes before any of them would have to be onstage.

The first step was to set the trap. As everybody knows, when you're setting a trap, there are two things you need to think about: what bait to use and where to put it. For instance, if you want to catch a tiger, you have to lure him in with the things he likes to eat, like a tasty wild boar. And then you have to put the boar in a place tigers like to hang out.

Micah, Armin, and Lydia knew that the thief they were trying to catch seemed to hang out around the auditorium, and he had a strange love of fifth-grade artwork and peanut butter sandwiches. It was an unusual combination, to be sure. But it was something they could work with.

The first thing they did was get into their costumes so they'd be ready as soon as Miss Petunia needed them onstage. Then they carefully placed Lydia's peanut butter sandwich and Armin's hand turkey in a back corner of the auditorium. Finally, they climbed up the long, metal ladder that hung from the catwalk.

This was no easy climb, even under the best of conditions. But when you happen to be dressed like an artichoke, it's extremely difficult. Add to that the fact that Micah was trying to carry a huge bag of snacks, and it's a wonder he got up there at all.

But up there he got, and then he immediately started unpacking his food onto the thin platform he'd be sharing with Lydia and Armin. He tried to be as quiet as possible. As he'd learned from Maxx Dryver, the key to a good stakeout was staying under the radar.

Lydia, in full cream of mushroom soup costume, came up right after him and sat down cross-legged, already staring down at the trap they'd set. Armin, the box of raisins, was not right on her heels.

"Come on, Armin," Lydia ecouraged. "You can do it! You're halfway there!"

Micah shook his head. "Seriously, man. You're not even carrying anything."

"Hey, give me a break," whispered Armin. "I don't pick on you for all the things you're scared of."

"Such as?" Micah asked defensively.

"Such as your neighbor's cat!"

"Hey! That was supposed to be a secret. And besides, he has fangs like a vampire!"

"Knock it off, you two," Lydia said, stretching her hand down to help Armin up the last few steps. "Let's all just enjoy our time together catching a thief."

"And eating snacks!" said Micah.

"Wow," Armin whispered, eyeing the spread on the platform. "Chips and salsa. Skittles. Salt and vinegar chips. Mustard pretzels. Chocolate chip cookies."

"What are those white things?" Lydia asked.

"Yogurt-covered Cheetos."

"That's disgusting."

"You've never even tried them." Micah opened the bag, grabbed a handful, and tossed them into his mouth—then nearly gagged. Lydia was right. Disgusting. They tasted the way wet gym shoes smell.

He looked over at Lydia, still staring fixedly at the trap they'd set. "You see anyone creeping around down there yet?"

"Nope."

Micah watched a kindergartner in a carrot costume at the back of the auditorium. But the kindergarten carrot didn't seem to notice the trap. Instead, he plopped down on the ground and rolled down the sloping aisle like a log rolling down a hill. Kindergartners are weird.

Things Kindergartners Do When They Think No One's Paying Attention

- Pick their nose

- Pick their friend's nose

- Taste all the gum under the auditorium seats to see which one still has the most flavor

- Climb up the stage curtain like a monkey going after a banana

- Accidentally tie their shoelace around a sleeve button when they're trying to tie their shoe, struggle to get untied, flip over on their back, and get stuck there like a turtle

- Sit in the corner, reading a Russian novel (This one only applies to Mindy St. John. She's kind of a nerd.)

"Hey, you dropped some Skittles," Armin whispered to Micah.

"That's okay. We've got plenty."

"I'm not worried about the Skittles. I'm worried about anyone who might be walking below you."

Suddenly, an extra head popped over the top of the ladder. "Hey guys! What's going on?" It was Gabe. He was in his gummy worm costume. "Shhh!" Micah whispered. "We're on a stakeout."

"Oh!" Gabe said. "I'm no good at stakeouts. I don't know how to be quiet. My mom says I'm too enthusiastic. Have fun!"

And just like that, he disappeared back down the ladder.

The others sat in silence for a few more seconds. Gabe was right. Being silent was hard.

"You think this is going to work?" Micah whispered.

"Probably not," Lydia whispered back.

"I thought you said this was a good idea," Armin said. He sounded annoyed.

"Actually, I just said it was the best idea we'd had yet. But that doesn't mean it was a good one."

"Well, I think we should test our DNA," Micah said.

"Whose DNA?"

"Everyone who will let us. The three of us. Gabe. Anyone who's willing in the play."

"Why would we test ours? You think one of us did this?" Lydia whispered.

"Probably not, but why not test it?"

"Probably not?" Armin snapped angrily.

"It's always best to make sure," Micah whispered. He swung himself sideways to get a better angle of their trap, accidentally knocking several salt and vinegar chips off the platform. He watched them drift slowly to the ground like leaves in autumn.

Micah heard Armin grumble beside him.

"What's up with you?" Micah asked him.

"I just can't believe all this ridiculous food you brought up here. It doesn't seem like you're taking this very seriously. It's like you just want to fool around and play a game of cops and robbers."

"Exactly!" Micah said. "This should be fun. You're taking it all way too seriously."

"Of course I'm taking it seriously," Armin shot back. "My art is at stake!"

"I think we've heard enough about your art by now," Lydia barked.

"You never really cared about my art, did you?" Armin yelled.

"Put a sock in it, Armin!" Lydia hissed. "You can always draw more pictures."

"Yeah. And you're just grumpy because you're hungry," Micah said.

"Of course I'm hungry! No sane person would eat this disgusting junk food you brought. And the lunch I brought from home is being used in your stupid trap!"

"My stupid trap?" Micah shouted. "I thought we were all in this together!"

The friends sat quietly thinking . . . or were they fuming? It was hard to tell.

Suddenly, another head popped over the top of the ladder. It was a stalk of celery this time. And not just any celery—unfortunately, it was the lead celery.

"Vat are you doing up here? This is no place for ze leads in ze play! Oh wait—zat's right. You're not ze leads in ze play. While I am ze lead celery, you're just regular cast members."

"If you have to know, we're on a stakeout," Armin said in exasperation. "We're trying to catch the thief that's been stealing stuff around here."

"I don't think it's verking. Everyone can hear you arguing all around ze whole auditorium. Vy don't you just hire a private investigator, like normal human beings vould do?"

"Because that would be insanely expensive," Lydia said.

"Oh yes. I keep forgetting. You're poor. How sad that must make you feel. Okay. I'll be going now. I just vanted you to know you look ridiculous up here."

Micah sighed. "Thanks."

Hanz disappeared back down the ladder.

"He's probably right," Micah admitted. "This is never going to work."

"Worst stakeout ever," said Armin.

"At least we still have some yummy snacks to bring home!"

Micah started to gather the goodies to put back in his bag. But just as he reached for the Skittles, his foot slipped off the edge of the platform. His leg started to slide down further, and in a panic, he grabbed at the railing.

He missed. Instead, all he got was a handful of mushy, wet salsa.

Now he was really panicking. With both hands he grabbed first at the slick platform underneath him. But there was nothing there to grip. His arms flailed in front of him as if he were swimming the front crawl, until at last, his fingers found the handrail on the other side. He was safe!

The salsa and tortilla chips were not so lucky.

Down they sailed, through the air, finally landing thirty feet below.

Even from high overhead in a dark auditorium, Micah could see the large puddle of red goop on the floor, surrounded by yellow flakes of tortilla chip.

For a moment, all was silent. Then suddenly, from every corner of the stage, kindergartners in vegetable costumes swarmed to the chips and salsa like wolves moving in for the kill. Nothing could be heard above the maniacal screams of "Five-second rule! Five-second rule!"

Within minutes, there was nothing left. No red puddle of goop. No tortilla chip crumbs. Just a clean carpet and dozens of well-fed kindergartners drifting back to their spots onstage.

By the end of rehearsal, Micah could still feel the tension between him and his friends, but at least they hadn't stopped talking to each other.

"You two heading straight home, or you want to hang out at the playground?" he asked.

"I could go for a swing," said Lydia. "It's been a long day. Probably good to unwind."

They climbed down the ladder to their trap, to pick up the uneaten sandwich and hand turkey, then headed for the seats where they'd put their book bags and coats. Micah had put all his stuff in one pile—his coat, his backpack, his lunch box, and even his extra pair of shoes that he'd brought for gym. (His mom had insisted he wear leather tie shoes to go with his new brown pants. Moms! What can you do?)

But as Micah looked around, he noticed that one thing wasn't in the pile.

"Do you see a gym shoe over there?" Micah asked Armin.

"Nope. Maybe it slipped through the folding seat onto the ground."

"It's not over here either," said Lydia.

Suddenly all three of them stared back and forth at one another, eyes wide in horror.

"He struck again!" Lydia said.

Micah nodded. "Right under our noses!"

Stakeout Strikeout

Ugh! I thought the stakeout was going to be fun, but it turned out awful. How could it be such a drag? The cops on TV always make it look like so much fun!

It probably would have been fun if we hadn't gotten into such a big fight. I don't get it. What's Armin so upset about, and why is Lydia so crabby? They're being ridiculous.

I think.

Or maybe I am. That often seems to be the case.

Armin and Lydia are my best friends, so we're going to have to work through this. They're completely worth it.

So let us try to do what makes peace and helps one another.
Romans 14:19 (ICB)

▷ **Have YOU ever had an argument with a good friend?**

▷ **What did YOU do to resolve it? What should Micah do to resolve the tension with his friends?**

CHAPTER SEVEN

Despite the circumstances, Micah decided to hang out at the playground anyway. Lydia was right—it would be good to unwind after a long day. Besides, he wasn't in any hurry to go home and explain to his mom and dad that someone had stolen one of his gym shoes.

The playground was hopping that afternoon. It seemed like everyone who was in rehearsal must've had the same idea about going there to relax. The older kids found places to sit—on swings, teeter-totters, monkey bars, and so on—and were talking over their day. PB and J were perched on the teeter-

totter, like true reporters hoping to catch the news of the day amidst the chaos of recess. Gabe and Frank were each on a swing, while Micah and Lydia were seated on top of the monkey bars, next to the swing set. Armin sat below them. He'd had enough heights for one day.

Meanwhile, most of the kindergartners were playing some kind of blindfolded freeze tag game while drilling each other with wood chips. The rest of the kindergartners were just eating wood chips.

"So, any new theories about who the thief is?" Frank asked. "By the way, I was sorry to hear about your missing shoe, Micah."

"Thanks," Micah said. Despite his popularity, Frank was one of the nicest kids in school. "Unfortunately, none of our thief-catching strategies have worked so far. He's always one step ahead of us. Any suggestions?"

"The thief seems pretty smart," yelled PB, who'd—amazingly—heard Micah and Frank's conversation over the squeak, squeak of the teeter-totter. "In fact, it could be a whole crew of thieves! It sounds like the work of organized crime."

"It didn't seem very organized to me," said Gabe. "They left scraps of paper everywhere!"

"I think PB is talking about the mob," Armin explained.

"Exactly," said PB. "The mob. The mafia. Cosa Nostra. Whatever you want to call them. They're behind everything these days! Maybe J and I should do some investigative journalism."

Lydia gave a disgusted grunt. "So," she said, "your theory is that the Mafia, who make millions of dollars on crime every year, couldn't resist stealing a kid's sketchbook, a peanut butter sandwich, and a left shoe?"

"Actually," said Micah. "It was my right shoe."

"Oh. That changes everything," Lydia muttered.

"Okay," said Frank. "We need to think about this logically. So far, we have a missing sketchbook, a missing peanut butter sandwich, and a missing shoe. What do all these things have in common?"

"They're all missing!" Gabe shouted.

Lydia sighed. "Other than that."

"It's hard to figure out much of a pattern," Armin said.

"Yeah. Who steals one shoe?" PB hollered as he teetered and tottered across from J. "There's no resale value in that."

All the other kids stared at him, dumbfounded.

"What? Criminals have to think about these things." He abruptly stopped seesawing and got off the teeter-totter, almost sending PB and J flying into the next county.

"Perhaps ze pattern is not in ze objects, but in ze

order of ze thefts," said Hanz, who had been waiting impatiently for either Gabe or Frank to vacate a swing.

"What are you talking about?" Micah said.

"First, Armin loses his sketchbook, like ze loser he is. Zen, he blames it on Lydia, so he steals her sandwich. She blames zat on you, so she steals your shoe. See! All ze puzzle pieces fit together! Crime solved!"

"That's ridiculous!" Lydia, Armin, and Micah all shouted at once.

But Micah glanced at Lydia and then at Armin out of the corner of his eye to see if they looked suspicious. Meanwhile, he noticed them glancing at him too. Did that mean they really were suspicious? Or did it mean they thought he was suspicious? Figuring out who looked suspicious wasn't as easy as Maxx Dryver made it seem!

Suddenly one of the blindfolded kindergartners ran right through their conversation. "It was probably a ninja!" she shouted.

Gabe stopped himself mid-swing. "That's what I've been saying all along!"

"Why would a ninja want to steal one shoe?" Armin asked.

The kindergartener stopped, lifted the blindfold off one of her eyes, and stared at Armin. "It was probably a ninja who always balances himself on his right foot so he can kick people with his left one."

"That's dumb."

"No, it's not! I know a guy like that!"

"No, you don't."

"I might!"

"It could be a one-legged alien," Gabe offered, back to swinging again. "They'd give anything for a right gym shoe. They're very rare in space."

Another kindergartner joined the first, this one staring at Micah. "What size shoe do you wear?"

"Why?"

"It might have been a Bigfoot who took your shoe."

"I'm a size 7. I don't think it was a bigfoot."

The two kindergartners looked at each other, giggled, and ran off.

Micah shook his head, then glanced over at Gabe, who was now holding his stomach. "All this crime solving is making my tummy hurt," Gabe complained.

"It's probably just from swinging," said Lydia. "You might want to stop."

Suddenly Gabe bent over, and his lunch shot out of his mouth like a geyser. "Too late," he said, wiping his mouth.

"Seriously?" Micah asked. "Just from swinging?"

Gabe shrugged. "I can't ride rides like I could when I was a kid."

A Partial List of the Things That Make Gabe Vomit

- Swinging
- Watching other people swing
- Sailing
- Flying
- Riding in a car
- Standing on one of those moving sidewalks at the airport that goes approximately three miles an hour
- The sight of blood
- The sight of Band-Aids, because they might have blood under them
- The sight of tomato soup, because it sort of looks like blood
- Watching other people vomit
- Watching himself vomit (it's a vicious cycle—his first vomit leads to a second vomit, then to a third, and so on)
- Lydia's whole wheat cranberry nut bars
- Anything with kale in it
- Cats dressed up like people

Everyone was stumped about the crime wave. Even Chet didn't seem to have any answers, and he knew crime better than anyone! Micah started to gather his stuff to head home for dinner, when he noticed a movement out of the corner of his eye, in the direction of the school. He glanced over and saw someone coming out of a little-used side door. It was a small, dark-haired boy in a baggy sweatshirt and baseball cap, carrying an awkwardly-shaped duffel bag. He was probably a kindergartner, based on his size. Micah didn't think he'd ever seen him before. He definitely wasn't in the play.

"Where does that door go to?" Micah asked.

"It goes outside!" Gabe said.

"No, I mean what room does it come from in the school?"

"I think it's the music room door," said Frank.

"Wait!" demanded Armin. "The music room is where we found some of the scraps of my sketchbook!"

"Yeah!" said Micah. "And doesn't that bag look weird? What do you think he's carrying in there? A shoe, perhaps?"

"I guess it could be," Lydia said. "But that's quite a leap. He just looks like a kid with a bag to me."

"A suspicious-looking kid with a suspicious-looking bag!" said Micah. "Don't you think he looks suspicious, Chet?"

Chet shrugged. "I could see that."

"I think we need to follow him and ask a few questions," Micah proposed. "Who's coming with me?"

Silence. Micah looked from face to face, but no one was meeting his eye. "Frank? PB? J? Hanz? Lydia?"

Still no one volunteered.

Except Gabe. "Can I come? I've always wanted to be in a chase scene. And chasing people doesn't even make me vomit! Usually."

Micah sighed. Gabe was not his first choice for a high-speed rundown. "Sure. I guess so." He kept looking around the circle. "What about you, Chet? You'll help, right? You said yourself you think he looks suspicious!"

Chet shook his head. "Yeah, but the problem is, I'm usually on the side of crime. It would go against my code to try to stop it."

Hard to argue with that.

"Armin? You'll help me, right?"

Armin stared at him. Micah had no idea what he'd say. They'd had some rocky times together lately. Finally, Armin nodded.

"Fine. I'll come. But you better not do anything stupid! This isn't just cops and robbers."

Micah took off after the kid before Armin could change his mind. "Don't worry. It'll be fun!"

"That's not the point!" Armin shouted.

But Micah was already too far ahead to hear.

Micah felt so free! So alive! He chased the suspect across the playground field like he was a lion chasing an antelope across the Serengeti. But not a regular old antelope, a really mean antelope, who stole stuff from innocent people, like . . . you know . . . sketchbooks and shoes and delicious peanut butter sandwiches.

The kindergartner (if that's really what he was, and not just some kind of secret identity), didn't notice Micah at first. By the time Micah started running, the kid was already at the far side of the field, walking at a normal pace, just like he was completely innocent. This kid was good! But just as the kid stepped off the field onto the sidewalk, he turned his head, noticing Micah coming after him. Suddenly, he took off like his pants were on fire!

Micah watched him run down the sidewalk and turn onto the first street on his right—Lincoln Avenue. Micah glanced behind him to check on Armin and Gabe. Armin wasn't too far back. He was faster than Micah and was gaining on him quickly.

Gabe, on the other hand, was no more than fifty feet across the playground field and already holding his side.

"I'm cramping up! I'm cramping up!" Gabe shouted. "You got a banana?"

"Why would I have a banana?"

"For the cramps."

"It's just a stitch," Micah shouted back. "Just push through it. You'll be fine."

"Go on without me!"

"We will," Micah answered. He didn't even pause to think about it.

Micah turned onto Lincoln Avenue with Armin now running by his side. The kindergartner was just on the other side of the hot dog stand, still a block ahead. But Armin and Micah were gaining ground. Micah looked over to get Armin's attention, then did that thing where you point to your eyes with two fingers and then point to something else.

"What does that mean?" Armin asked.

"No idea," Micah said. "But, man, it sure looks cool when Maxx Dryver does it!"

Even running full speed, Armin managed to roll his eyes.

Suddenly the kindergartner turned left down an alley behind the big, brick NationBank building. By the time Micah and Armin had made the turn behind him, he was halfway up a fire escape.

"You go around the other side," said Micah. "I'll climb after him."

Armin wasn't going to argue. Micah figured the fire escape ladder looked a bit too shaky for someone who's scared of heights. Micah grabbed onto the first rung of the ladder, five feet above the ground. He swung himself up and started to climb.

As it turned out, it was even a bit shaky for someone who's not scared of heights. Or maybe it was just that Micah's arms were shaking because he wasn't used to this kind of exercise. Either way, the climbing didn't get any easier the higher he went.

The bank was three stories high, but to Micah it felt like each story was taller than the last. Was that even possible? Could some cruel architect have designed the building that way on purpose to taunt kids who were chasing other kids up fire escapes? It seemed unlikely, but Micah wasn't willing to rule it out.

At last he got to the top and swung his legs up onto the roof. It was a large, flat surface with

one small, brick structure in the center and several pipes and vents popping out here and there and everywhere. Micah looked around and didn't see anyone else at first. But then he spotted movement to his left. He turned to catch a quick glimpse of a small, dark-haired head disappearing over the edge. Micah ran over and followed him down another fire escape.

Glancing down, he could see the boy would soon have nowhere to go. He was trapped in a dead-end alley! On one side was a wire fence ten feet high, stretching all the way across the alley from the bank to the Shop-and-Save, Micah's second favorite store (after Shazam Video Games, of course). On the other side was Armin.

Micah wasn't more than ten feet above the kindergartner's head when he got to the bottom. He watched the kid glance toward Armin, then dart forward in the direction of the fence. There was nowhere to escape!

Then Micah heard a sound that was music to his

ears. Police sirens! Somebody must have seen the chase and called for backup! This was the greatest thing ever! Not only was he going to catch a thief; he was going to do it with real, live cops watching and admiring his work!

Micah took off after the kindergartner, who was now clawing up the fence like a dumpster-diving raccoon. The kid was no more than four feet off the ground when Micah caught up to him, grabbed him by the ankles, and yanked down as hard as he could. In his head he pictured himself pulling the suspect to the ground and onto his belly. He'd look awesome as he held the kid's arms behind his back until the cops came to cuff him.

Instead, as he yanked the kid off the fence with all his strength, he fell backwards onto the pavement. Somehow Micah ended up on his back, with the kindergartner lying on top of him. Armin hurried over and jumped on top of the kindergartner and held on for dear life, like he was recovering a fumbled football in the Super Bowl.

Sure, maybe the whole thing looked a little awkward, but who cares? They got their man!

The sirens grew louder and louder until the police lights filled up the alley. Three cop cars squealed to a stop a few feet from the small stack of children on the ground.

Micah couldn't believe how great this felt. He was a hero! And not just any old hero, a crime-fighting hero! Huge things were ahead of him!

First, he'd solve all of Middletown's unsolved mysteries! He'd figure out who stole the city's entire supply of tissues during hay fever season. (There wasn't a dry sleeve in town!) He'd catch the vandal who painted tiger stripes on Miss Moffet's Shih Tzu. (Muffy looked hideous. Like a sabertooth with an underbite.) And finally, he'd solve the puzzle of who took the last banana chocolate chip muffin from his mom's pantry. (Who was he kidding? That one was definitely Audrey.) The sky was the limit! He'd become an international man of mystery.

"What's going on here?" A gruff-voiced officer had gotten out of his squad car and marched up to the kids. "Break it up!"

Two other cops got out of their cars, one with a police dog barking in the general direction of the kid pile. Boy oh boy, Micah sure would hate to be a criminal in this town!

Lying on the bottom of the pile, Micah could feel Armin get off him, followed by the kindergartner. Micah himself stood up last, straight and proud. This was the moment where he'd get the recognition he deserved! A special badge of his own? An award from the mayor? A huge parade?

No, that last one was ridiculous. It would probably just be a small parade.

But his thoughts were broken up by the kindergartner. "Thank you, Mr. Policeman."

That was weird, Micah thought. Who ever heard of a criminal thanking a cop for arresting him?

"I'm glad somebody called us," said the policeman. "We don't put up with bullying in this town!"

Bullying? Micah wondered. *What does bullying have to do with anything? We're dealing with a thief.*

"Wait," Armin said to the kindergartner. "You called the cops? On yourself?"

"Actually, I told the hot dog man to call 911. My mom always says, 'If you ever feel stranger danger, call the police—they're your friends in blue!'"

The gruff-voiced policeman turned to Micah and Armin. "Why were you two chasing this boy? And what were you going to do when you caught him?"

"Uh . . . uh . . . ," Micah stammered.

"We thought . . . ," Armin started.

Suddenly the whole picture became clear to

Micah. He was a big kid chasing a little kid. He, Micah Murphy, was a bully! He was Chet! Is this how people ended up in a life of crime? It all started with a crazy mix-up?

But Micah could see it now—his whole life flashed before his eyes. He'd spend five to ten years in the slammer on bullying charges, and he'd have to learn to play gin rummy and the harmonica—and he probably couldn't even afford a cool harmonica, so he'd have to get some cheap plastic one with Dora the Explorer on it—until one day a cell buddy would hatch an escape plan that forced him to crawl through 500 yards of sewer pipes until they escaped to the Gulf of Mexico, where he'd have to work on a tuna boat and get a bunch of sailor tattoos—which would look ridiculous on his skinny arms—and wear a fake beard made out of cat hair and Elmer's glue.

No, that was no life for him!

Wow, Micah thought to himself. Thirty seconds ago, he was daydreaming of being a hero. Now everything was falling apart. His mom was right: some days his emotions really were all over the place.

"We're so sorry, sir!" Micah shouted. "We didn't mean to bully anyone! We thought this kid stole my shoe!"

The police officers all looked down at Micah's feet.

"Not these shoes. A gym shoe."

"Why would you think he stole your shoe?"

"Look at his bag!" Micah said. "He was coming

out of the music room carrying it. It looks suspicious, right?"

The kid opened up his bag and pulled out a long, thin musical instrument. "This is just my oboe."

"Oh," said Micah.

"O-boe," the kid repeated.

"I heard you," Micah said. He was in no mood to be taught new vocabulary words by a kindergartner.

The first police officer turned back to the kindergartner. "What do you think? Just a misunderstanding, or you want me to take them in for questioning?"

The kindergartner looked Micah and Armin up and down. "I think we can let them off with a warning."

The three cops looked at one another with raised eyebrows. "So warned," said the second one.

"Hey guys! How's it going?" Gabe had finally caught up to them, still holding the cramp in his side, grinning ear to ear.

"Fine!" Armin said. He didn't sound fine at all, but Gabe didn't seem to notice. In fact, he didn't seem to notice much of anything about what was going on.

"What a great chase scene, huh?" Gabe said. "That was awesome!"

"No, actually it wasn't," said the gruff-voiced police officer.

"It wasn't?"

"No, it wasn't. It was a waste of our time and yours."

"Oh." Gabe looked slightly disappointed. But only slightly. "We'll do better next time."

"Please don't ever do something like this again," said the cop.

"Okay. We won't chase anyone down unless we're really sure next time."

"Even then."

"But you'll give us a private number where we can call in tips, right?"

"There is no private number."

"Oh, I get it. You have to pretend there's not a private number so it stays a secret."

"No. That's not what I meant."

"But at least you're going to give us deputy badges, right?"

"No."

"Can we ride in your car and turn on your siren?"

"No."

"Can I pet your dog?"

"No."

Gabe looked at him and winked. "We'll talk."

The cop sighed and walked back to his squad car.

Armin, Gabe, and Micah walked back to the school playground to get their stuff before heading home.

"That was humiliating," said Armin.

"It wasn't the best," Micah admitted.

"I can't believe you talked me into chasing that kid down."

"Well, we had to do something!"

"No, we didn't! Nothing would have been better than something!"

"But I thought you wanted to get your sketchbook back!"

"Absolutely! I just want to do it smartly. Not like we're little kids pretending to be some hero from TV. Sometimes I think you stole my sketchbook just so you could have fun solving a crime!"

Micah couldn't believe Armin had said that! Here he was, trying to help, and he gets accused of stealing. "That doesn't even make sense! Then why would my shoe go missing?"

"I don't know. Maybe to make it look like you were innocent."

By this time they were at the playground. Lydia was still there, waiting for them and watching their stuff. "I wish you two would stop arguing, get your stuff, and head home. I'm starving!"

"Stop complaining about how hungry you are," said Armin. "If you ate normal food, you'd be full and happy like the rest of us."

"See if I help you out anymore," Lydia said. "Besides, more and more I'm starting to think Hanz was right—you just lost your sketchbook in the first place."

"Forget it," Armin shouted. "I'm out of here!"

"Me too!" Lydia shouted.

"Me too!" Micah shouted.

Gabe smiled and waved. "I'm out of here too! See you tomorrow!"

When Micah got home, he was in a terrible mood. It must have been obvious from the look on his face as soon as he came through the door. "What's wrong?" his dad asked.

"Someone stole my shoe!"

His dad, mom, and sister all looked down at his feet.

Micah sighed. "Not these shoes! My gym shoe."

"How do you lose a shoe?" asked his mom.

"I didn't lose it. Somebody stole it."

"Why would anyone steal one shoe?" asked Audrey.

"Ahhhh!!!!" Micah couldn't take anymore. He threw his hands in the air and stomped off to his room. He looked at his computer for a split second before deciding not to vlog about how the investigation went that day. Some things were just too real to share with his fans.

Stumped

Well, that could have ended in disaster! How was I supposed to know that sneaky kindergartener was innocent? He looked pretty guilty to me.

Another dead end. I've got to admit it, I'm stumped. We're all stumped. No one knows who stole Armin's sketchbook . . . and Lydia's lunch . . . and my gym shoe. Who steals one, stinky shoe?!

I almost got arrested for bullying a six-year-old. I would never do that!

I can't think straight. This mystery is driving me crazy. And worse, I'm afraid it's tearing me and my friends apart.

Those who trust in their own insight are foolish, but anyone who walks in wisdom is safe. Proverbs 28:26 NLT

 Why do YOU think this stressful situation is hurting Micah's ability to think straight?

 What do YOU think Micah should do to help him focus?

CHAPTER EIGHT

One week later, Micah, Armin, and Lydia were no closer to solving the crimes. They were also no closer to each other. Their friendship was on the rocks, and everybody knew it. Whenever they were together, there was a coldness between them that was so obvious, even Gabe could sniff it out. And Gabe's tension radar was generally set to zero. (Hanz, meanwhile, took full credit for the problems in their friendship, which somehow put each of them in an even fouler mood).

It's not like they were giving each other the silent treatment—that was something only little kids did. (The silent treatment was for fourth graders. It would be downright embarrassing at their age.) But everything always seemed tense when they were around each other.

They just didn't smile and laugh together anymore. Not even when Chet got his hand stuck in the restroom towel dispenser (a first grader had told him he'd put his lunch money up there for safe keeping). Or when Gabe ate all the turnip hash leftovers, then threw it up all over the teeter-totter. And one of the soccer goals. And the monkey bars. And somehow, on Hanz's shoes.

No, life just wasn't as funny when you didn't have friends to laugh with.

But the end of the week was here, and that meant opening night of the musical. For weeks the posters had been hanging all over the school, and the advertisements had been playing on all the local radio stations. There was even a huge announcement in removable letters on the sign in front of the school. It originally had read, "Opening Night for

'Don't You Carrot All?'" But of course, it only took a few days for somebody to rearrange the letters. By the time the play arrived, it said, "Opening Night for 'roll A Donut YaC rot.'" Which makes no sense at all. Unless you're a second grader. In which case, it's hilarious.

On Friday night Micah sat in a chair backstage with a towel wrapped around his neck. There is never a good reason to be sitting in a chair with a towel wrapped around your neck. Best-case scenario, you're getting a haircut. It's not fun, but if all goes well, you'll be out of there in fifteen minutes and won't look too embarrassing. A second option is you're at the dentist. Your mouth is being stretched out like a water balloon, and someone's stabbing your gums with sharp sticks while lecturing you for not flossing.

But there's a much worse scenario than either of these. If you're an eleven-year-old boy, the scariest reason to be sitting in a chair with a towel wrapped around your neck is because someone is putting makeup on you. There's no way this won't turn into long-term embarrassment. Maybe even a humiliating nickname. Ugh.

"Are you sure this is necessary, Mrs. Millwood?" Micah asked his makeup artist, who happened to be Frank Millwood's mom. She was kindly volunteering to help get the kids all ready, so he hated to be too grumpy to her.

"Of course it's necessary! You can't go onstage without makeup. Didn't anyone tell you that when you signed up for the play?"

"It must've been lost in the fine print."

"Well, if I do say so myself, you look fabulous! This is absolutely the best artichoke makeup I've ever done in my life!"

"How many times in your life have you done artichoke makeup?" Micah asked.

"Just once so far," Mrs. Millwood admitted. "But I'm guessing I'll get all the Hollywood artichoke gigs after they see this."

Classic Movies That Could Have Been Food-Based, but Sadly, Were Not
• Cherry Poppins
• Tofu Panda
• Soy Story 2
• Lord of the Onion Rings
• Harry Butter and the Half-Baked Shrimps
• Beauty and the Feast
• The Empire Likes Snacks
• The Eggo Movie

She passed a hand mirror over to Micah so he could take a look. She'd painted pointy green leaves all over his face, all angled upward, kind of like the skin of a pineapple. It matched perfectly with the rest of his costume. He'd looked at plenty of photos of artichokes since he'd gotten the part, and it looked exactly like the pictures.

In fact, to Micah's surprise, he loved it! When he'd heard someone would be doing his makeup, he was worried she'd make him look all fancy and pretty, like a girl. But he actually looked more like a hideous space creature or a terrifying swamp monster come to life. Awesome! Those were two of the least-embarrassing things he could ever hope to become!

All of a sudden, Micah was starting to get into the spirit of the night. He was feeling himself transform. Becoming one with the artichoke. He couldn't wait to get out there onstage and belt his song lyrics to the rafters. There would never be a better artichoke in an elementary school presentation of a food-based musical in all of world history!

He jumped out of the chair, ripped the towel from around his neck, and threw it on the ground. He'd pick it up later, but for now, he had a job to do!

Micah marched down the hallway to the stage. He listened to the band play the notes of the opening number as excitement built in his chest.

Three! Two! One!

He burst through the curtain and onto the stage! The bright lights blinded him as he lifted his arms over his head to belt out the opening number.

This was his chance of a lifetime! A golden opportunity to wow the crowd like they'd never been wowed before! He took a deep breath and opened his mouth wide to sing to the rafters!

Then suddenly he remembered he wasn't supposed to be onstage until act 2.

Micah sat by himself on a bench in the hallway beside the auditorium. He'd have to work himself back up to wanting to get out there in front of the crowd again. Hopefully he'd be ready by the second act. Gabe slithered up to him in his gummy worm sleeping bag alongside Armin in his raisin box and Hanz in his celery tube. They all sat down in the huddle of seats around Micah.

"Vell done," Hanz said. "Zat vas quite a debut."

"It could happen to anyone," Gabe said sympathetically.

"Really?" asked Armin. "To me that seems like the sort of huge, embarrassing mistake Micah specializes in."

"Whatever," Micah said. Best comeback ever.

Lydia, as cream of mushroom soup, came up to them with her bowl around her waist and her face painted creamy white with brown spots.

Armin turned to her. "You look like something the lunch room cooked up."

Lydia looked his raisin box costume up and down. "What are those little brown spots coming out of your costume? Mouse droppings?"

Hanz shrugged and stood up to walk away. "I see zat my verk here is done."

Micah looked at Lydia and Armin. "How about

we just sit here in silence and listen to the play until it's our time to go onstage."

"You sure you even know when that is?" asked Lydia.

Micah ignored her.

The lyrics toward the end of the first act wafted backstage. The scene was a hip-hop battle between two gangs of foods that didn't get along. They were on either side of the stage, snapping their fingers and glaring at each other. The first gang was made up of potatoes, carrots, beef-flavored tofu, and a pot of boiling herb water. They rapped at the other group:

We don't want you in our stew!

We don't care for foods like you!

The last thing that we'd ever do

Is try to cook up something new!

The other gang was made up of eggs, spinach, mushrooms, and cheddar cheese. They shot back:

We don't want you in our omelet
Cookin' up breakfast—yep, we're on it!
Foods like you would make us vomit
Wish more things would rhyme with omelet

(Micah always thought that last line was a bit of a cop-out, despite the fact that it was true. But apparently even Miss Petunia's creativity had its limits.)

He stood up. "Okay, it's about time for act 2. We should probably get ready to go."

Lydia, Armin, and Gabe got up to follow him without saying a word. He wondered how they'd all perform once they got onstage together. He figured having cast members hating each other wasn't the ideal condition for performing together. But he could be wrong—he was certainly no expert.

Before going to the edge of the curtain to make his second debut of the night, he looked himself over in a tall, stand-up mirror that was there for the actors to check over their costumes and makeup one last time. He was practically unrecognizable. Green from head to foot, and with his face covered in painted-on leaves, it was hard to figure out the expression on his face, let alone see how he was feeling inside.

How was he feeling inside?

Embarrassed. Annoyed. Lonely.

Those did not seem like the kind of emotions that would energize a big, successful performance. But maybe that was the point of acting. You don't show the audience what you're really feeling. You show them what you want them to see. He could rise above and give the audience their money's worth! The show must go on!

Now he was getting his mojo back. He was starting to feel it again. He was a hideous space creature! A terrifying swamp monster! The greatest artichoke Hollywood had ever seen!

The lights went up on act 2, and he burst out from behind the curtain. He began the quick, purposeful march to his spot on stage left and felt himself beginning to seize the moment. The lights were bright! The crowd was his! The band played the first notes of act 2, and he took the last step to his spot.

And that's when his right heel found a small, Styrofoam olive that must've fallen out of somebody's costume. His foot slipped out from under him and he fell flat on his big, puffy artichoke bottom.

Seriously?

Again?

Ugh!

He really needed to work on his entrances.

But then he felt a different emotion well up from deep within. He was no longer embarrassed. Or simply annoyed. No, now he was downright angry! He felt the passion of the moment spring up within him, and he was once again ready to belt songs out to the rafters!

The first song was about food that wanted to be so much more than what was expected of it. It was about overcoming obstacles and shooting for the stars. Anything can happen if you work hard enough and dream big enough!

As Micah's eyes adjusted to the lights, he could start to see people he knew in the crowd: his mom and dad, Audrey, his grandparents, Mr. Turtell, Miss Tinker, Dennis. He took a deep breath and sang at the top of his lungs:

I've got big dreams! Someday you'll see!
They'll put me in a brand new recipe!

The song went back and forth between several foods that always ended up being used in the same meals time after time. They were bored and felt like they needed to branch out. Lydia sang about how cream of mushroom soup wasn't just for casseroles. Armin sang about how he wanted to be in more than just oatmeal and breakfast cereals. Why did his snooty cousin, the Craisin, get to be in salads, but not him?

Then it was Micah's turn. He sang about how artichokes could be so much more than just a filler ingredient in spinach dip and an occasional pizza topping. He was tasty and had a lovely texture! He'd be great on a sandwich! Or as an after-school snack!

As they danced a two-step/jazz hands/hokey pokey combo, they all joined together once more in the big chorus:

We don't have to stay in our boring old roles
We can work together and reach brand new goals!

The applause rolled on and on, and Micah felt like he owned the place.

After the song ended, the script called for all the foods onstage to talk about how they could help one another branch out and reach new heights of popularity and flavor innovation.

"I think you'd make a wonderful gravy," said a radish to a carton of chocolate milk.

"If you want to be in a soup, you should totally go for it!" said a pine nut to a banana.

"I bet you'd taste really great on a sandwich!" the artichoke was supposed to say to the box of raisins.

But it didn't.

Instead, without thinking, Micah found himself saying, "I bet you'd taste really disgusting on a sandwich!"

Did he really just say that? Out loud? What was he thinking?

Maybe it was because he was mad at Armin, and it came out in an unplanned way. Or maybe it was the fact that raisins would, in fact, taste gross on a sandwich. Either way, now it was out of his mouth and he couldn't take it back. The damage was done.

Micah looked at Armin's face and saw him glaring right back at him. The raisin box was supposed to talk next. But he paused first, narrowing his eyes at Micah.

"Well, I think artichokes ruin a perfectly good pizza!"

That cranked it up a notch! It wasn't even close to the right line!

"Well, I think the artichoke and the box of raisins need to grow up," said the cream of mushroom soup.

Micah wasn't supposed to be the next one to speak, but by this time he didn't even care. "Well, I think the cream of mushroom soup needs to stop bossing us around!"

"Well, I wouldn't have to boss you around if raisins were less whiny and artichokes were less immature!"

"Well, I hope the artichoke and the cream of mushroom soup end up in a garbage disposal!"

The box of raisins charged the artichoke and

tackled him like a linebacker. Lying on the stage, the artichoke grabbed the box of raisins around the legs and pulled him down—right on top of him.

Micah could feel the corner of the raisin box stab into his left foot, and he yelled out in pain. Armin, meanwhile, was stuck on his back, waving his arms and legs around in a desperate attempt to stand himself back up.

The cream of mushroom soup rushed over, yanking the raisins off the artichoke.

The box of raisins stood up, glared at the cream of mushroom soup, and stomped off the stage.

The scene wasn't supposed to be over yet, but all the other foods didn't know what to do next. None of their lines now made any sense, so each and every one of them marched offstage after the raisins.

Their rousing chorus of being able to work together to reach bigger goals had been proven a lie. Their hopes were dashed. Now all they wanted to do was get out of there.

"So," said Miss Petunia to the cast backstage.

"Overall it was a worthy performance. There were some . . . er . . . improvised scenes here and there. Especially, it seemed, in act 2."

Micah could feel his face redden. He didn't want to meet Miss Petunia's eyes.

She went on. "Improvisation can be effective at times, and I certainly don't want to stifle any of my young geniuses in their creative process. That said, I'm not sure I completely understood the interpretation of the scene, particularly by the artichoke, the raisins, and the mushroom soup. But we can discuss that later. For now, get some rest, and we'll be back at it tomorrow night!"

Micah had already taken his costume and makeup off and headed straight to his parents, waiting in the back of the auditorium. He didn't want to talk to anyone. A nauseating blend of anger, shame, and exhaustion washed over him, and he was just glad to get out of there.

As they walked to their minivan, his mom put her arm around his shoulder. "That was . . . interesting."

His dad nodded. "It was a bit darker than usual for one of Miss Petunia's plays."

Audrey just stared at them in disbelief. "Are you kidding me? That was amazing!"

Micah assumed she was being sarcastic, which was usually a safe bet. But then she went on.

"It was so raw! So authentic! Micah, I didn't know you had that kind of passion in you!"

"Actually—" Micah started.

But she cut him off. "The way your character saw through all the fake 'niceness' and got right to the heart of the matter: that society is cruel and unfair!"

"But I was supposed to—"

"And then when the box of raisins snapped back with an insult to your very essence as an artichoke . . . Brilliant!"

"He wasn't really—"

"And the cream of mushroom soup! How she took control of the situation, calling society out for its childishness! It was just so perfect for today's political climate."

"But that part—"

"I confess, Micah, I didn't know you had this kind of raw honesty in you! I used to think you were just a goofball, but now I see that deep down inside . . . you're a true artist!"

Micah sighed. There was just too much to explain, and it didn't feel worth it. Let her have her moment of being proud of him. It was bound to come to a natural end before long.

But she was staring at him with loving pride, awaiting some brilliant response.

He'd best keep it brief.

"Yep. We were authentic, all right."

Well, at least he didn't lie.

A Little Help, Please?

Wow! I really humiliated myself in front of everyone tonight. (Except Audrey—I have no idea what she was talking about!) I wish I could start from scratch and do it all over again.

Of course, I can get over being embarrassed (I've had lots of practice). The bigger issue is, my friends are so mad at me right now. I don't remember ever fighting like this with Armin and Lydia before. Sure, we've argued now and then, but never like this. I just hope we can work it out. I can't lose them.

It's a good thing God is into healing relationships. I'm going to ask Him what to do next.

There are "friends" who destroy each other, but a real friend sticks closer than a brother. Proverbs 18:24 NLT

▷ **Have YOU ever felt like you might lose a friendship? What did you do?**

▷ **Do YOU think God cares about our friendships? What kind of friend does He want us to be?**

CHAPTER NINE

Micah's Saturday afternoon had been the most boring weekend afternoon he'd ever had in his whole life. What a waste. Saturday was the day he looked forward to all week. Those lazy afternoons were supposed to be about hanging out with friends and feeling free to run around and have fun. Instead, he spent all day moping.

Surprisingly, moping took a lot out of him. He was exhausted by the time his mom told him he needed to get going for the play. Miss Petunia had told them they were supposed to be there two hours before the musical started, to get dressed, get in makeup, and get in character. That was way too early. It would take him five minutes to get his costume on, fifteen minutes for Mrs. Millwood to do the makeup, and an infinite amount of time to get in character (he just didn't see it happening tonight). But his mom insisted on doing what Miss Petunia had asked of them.

Micah's mom dropped him off at the door, and the first person he saw was his fifth-grade teacher, Mr. Turtell.

"Hello, Mr. Murphy."

Mr. Turtell often called students by their last names. Micah wasn't sure why, but he didn't mind. It made him feel grown-up, which wasn't a common feeling for him lately.

"Hello, Mr. Turtell. Are you helping with the play tonight?"

"I volunteered to take tickets. I don't think I could do much more than that to help out with the school plays. To tell you the truth, I've never really understood the theater very well."

Micah wasn't very surprised to hear this. Mr. Turtell had a reputation as a stickler for rules, and he wasn't much for "thinking outside the box." So, figuring out the deep meanings in creative things, like song lyrics and plays, wasn't exactly his strength.

Mr. Turtell went on. "I came to last night's production, and I couldn't make heads or tails of it! I'm sure it was about something, but I had no idea what. What was the deeper meaning?"

Micah didn't really want to talk about last night's performance. "Maybe there wasn't a deeper meaning. Sometimes what you see is what you get!"

Mr. Turtell shook his head. "No. In the world of theater—especially in Miss Petunia's brilliant productions—there's always a deeper meaning!"

Micah didn't know what to say to this, but luckily Mr. Turtell didn't always need someone else to participate in his conversations.

"Perhaps it's about capitalism," said Mr. Turtell. "Or communism. Or populism. Or astigmatism. Or the Dewey decimal system."

Micah had no idea what he was talking about. He glanced around for a way out of this conversation, but no one was coming to his rescue. So, he just smiled and nodded as Mr. Turtell went on.

"Could it be about health care? Or the environment? Or animal rights? Specifically, why will turtles never be as accepted in society as dogs? Speaking of which, why doesn't anyone keep weasels as pets? You ever wondered that?"

Out of the corner of his eye, Micah noticed a small slip of paper caught in the grate of a heating vent, blowing in the draft. Could it be a torn piece of one of Armin's sketches? Probably not, but he had to make sure.

"Sorry, Mr. Turtell, but I've got to take off." Micah walked away and headed to the vent on the other side of the lobby.

Mr. Turtell didn't seem to notice. Micah could still hear him mumbling to himself. "Or maybe it's about the state of education. Or road construction. Or the decline of polka music. Or about how all-you-can-eat Chinese buffets always seem to run out of kung pao chicken."

Sure enough, the torn strip of paper in the vent was one of Armin's. Right away, Micah recognized the pencil work. He also recognized the subject of the portrait. It was Lydia, and it looked amazing! He couldn't believe how well Armin had captured her smile.

But where had the paper come from? It didn't

make sense for the thief to put it there on purpose. Had he just torn up the whole sketchbook and dumped it in the vents throughout the school? But why?

Micah walked from the lobby into the lunchroom. He knew there were several vents in there. He remembered because one time Hanz hid a bunch of limburger cheese in them as a practical joke. The lunchroom smelled like feet for weeks!

He bent down to investigate the vent closest to the door and didn't see anything at first. But it seemed like he heard something. A very quiet scraping sound. Bending down even lower, he stared into the vent until he could just see a tiny edge of paper rustling against the metal as the breeze from the duct made it shake like a leaf.

It wasn't easy to pull it out of there, but eventually he managed to grab hold of it with the tips of his fingers. Bingo! Another edge of a sketch. This one was too small for him to recognize its subject. But there were two more vents in the lunchroom, and

Micah decided to go and take a look at each of them. Sure enough, there were tons more strips of paper in them. The strips were too deep to reach in the second vent, but not so much in the third vent. He worked as best he could to retrieve several strips and looked them over carefully, piecing them together like a jigsaw puzzle.

Wait! That was his own face staring back at him! Armin had drawn a portrait of him? He had no idea. And it was amazing! Micah had always hated himself in pictures, but Armin's drawing made him look happy and confident. Almost cool.

A wave of regret washed over him. He realized that Armin wasn't just being whiny and overly sensitive. This sketchbook was personal to him! It wasn't just a bunch of drawings. It was time and memories and friendship.

And Micah had turned it all into a joke. He'd just wanted to pretend to be a hero. He'd wanted to play the role of Maxx Dryver, solving the case and bringing down the bad guys. Meanwhile, Armin was sad because he'd lost something very important to him.

And Lydia—well, she was right all along. Micah had been immature. Sure, Lydia and Armin had gone along with some of his strategies, but they were probably just trying to humor him. Until they got sick of it. Which he deserved.

But now maybe Micah could actually do something useful. Maybe some of the pages were still safe, and he could find them. He still couldn't put the whole mystery together just yet, but at least now he felt confident that the vents were full of bits and pieces of Armin's art. And that seemed like a great lead.

Was there a big pile of sketchbook pages—and maybe even his shoe—somewhere along the ducts and vents in the school? Was there a source where all the little bits and pieces were blowing from?

Micah needed to think. If bits of paper were somehow being blown through the school, he needed to figure out where the stream of air was coming from. This sounded too hard for him to figure out—he wasn't very handy when it came to understanding how things work, things like bikes and cars and houses.

But maybe it wasn't really all that complicated. Hot air was blowing through the vents, and hot air had to come from a heater, right? In other words, a furnace.

The furnace room!

It was no slam dunk, but he had to give it a try. The only thing was, he wasn't exactly sure where the school kept the furnace room. Every building had to have one, but where? He hadn't seen it in his day-to-day wanderings through the school. So what parts of the school did he never see? Were there any secret doors or passages? None that he'd noticed.

But then suddenly he remembered something. Not something he'd seen, but something he'd heard. Whispers. Rumors of a dark place where no one was allowed to go.

The basement.

Kids claimed to have ventured there before, but they never came back with proof. No pictures. No evidence. Probably just false bragging to make themselves sound brave to others.

But now Micah wondered. If it really existed, it would be the perfect place to keep a furnace. But how to find it?

All the kids who'd claimed to have gone there said there was only one way. Only one door and one set of steps, and it was in the kitchen. The kitchen was another place Micah had never set foot. But not because it was scary—or at least not in the same way.

You know the old saying about how you never want to see "how the sausage is made"? Imagine how much worse it would be to see how the turnip hash is made. Or the lima bean egg rolls. Micah's stomach turned over just thinking about some of the nightmarish concoctions the lunch ladies dreamed up.

But now he had no choice. Before he could talk himself out of it, he marched across the lunchroom and pushed through the swinging doors that led to the kitchen.

It was dark in there, and part of Micah wanted to keep it that way. The less he saw, the easier it would be to wipe the images from his mind. But he had to turn on the lights if he wanted to find the door to the basement.

He found a set of switches by the lunchroom door and flipped them on.

He took a sharp breath in. Little black things scurried across the floor and walls, looking for shadows to hide in. And what were those wood-and-metal contraptions on the counters and floor? They looked like mouse traps, but way too huge. Rat traps, maybe? They looked big enough to take down a badger.

A Few Things You Absolutely Do Not Want to See in Your School's Kitchen

- Rat traps
- Hairnet slingshots
- Toenail clippers
- Used strands of dental floss
- Large plastic tubs with labels that say "meat" but don't get any more specific than that
- Hazmat suits

Micah forced himself to focus. He didn't need to see any more of this; he just needed to find a door down to the lower level.

He walked to the back of the kitchen and saw three doors. One said "Exit," which probably led to the outside. One said "Freezer." That was self-explanatory. And the last one was unmarked. He turned the handle and tried to open it as quietly as possible.

Bingo! A wooden staircase led down into the darkness below. He flipped on the lights at the top of the steps. Now he just had to get up the courage to walk down.

It would be fine. It's not like there was some crazy monster that lived in an elementary school basement, waiting for kids to show up.

Ha! That was crazy. Right?

Of course. There were no such thing as monsters.

Or aliens.

Or ninjas.

Actually, ninjas were real. He'd have to keep an eye out for those.

Micah took a deep breath and stepped down the stairs slowly. Right, left, right, left. Wow, the basement was a long way down.

At last he got to the bottom and looked around. It really stunk down there! It smelled like his aunt's house, with all the cats and uncleaned litter boxes.

Even with the lights on, the room was dim and shadowy. It was a huge space with concrete walls, and the bare lightbulbs hanging from the ceiling didn't reach into all the corners. Then suddenly, in the bad lighting, Micah realized something. He'd been looking around for the thief's stash but had completely forgotten about the thief! What if he was down here right now, protecting his loot? He could be hiding in the shadows, waiting to pounce.

But Micah just had to press on. If he could find the remains of Armin's sketchbook, maybe he'd be able to somehow patch up their friendship.

For some reason Micah expected it to be silent in the basement, but there was a constant humming noise. Could that be from the furnace? Doing his best to ignore cobwebs and shadows, he made his way toward the sound on his left. Soon he came up to an enormous metal box, bigger than his bedroom, with huge pipes and tubes coming out of it like it was some kind of robot octopus.

This had to be it, right? It seemed as furnace-like as it could get. But now what was Micah supposed to do?

He looked around at the various parts of the machine, trying to figure out what he was even supposed to be looking for. But then he turned a corner and went around to the back of the furnace.

What he saw wasn't at all what he expected, but now it all made sense! How could he have been so stupid? What a relief! The mystery was solved as two beady little eyes stared back at him from on top of its treasure trove.

But before he even had a chance to collect his thoughts, he heard loud noises behind him. Then more noises coming from his right. Footsteps! And they were running right at him!

He wasn't supposed to be down there in the basement, and now he was trapped. He looked around for a place to hide, but there was no time. Two bright flashlights shined on his face, blinding him.

Micah threw his hands up in the air.

"I'm sorry! I know I shouldn't be here!"

Perspective is Everything

I'm finally starting to see things from Armin's perspective. He was really hurt that his sketchbook was stolen—he'd put a lot of time and effort into it, and it was personal to him. And there I was, more concerned about how much fun I was having playing Detective Micah, than being there for my friend.

Maybe I can make it up to him. Hopefully he'll forgive me for not paying attention to how he was feeling. Paying attention isn't one of my strengths. But I guess it's something for me to work on!

It's a good thing Armin is such a forgiving friend.

Be kind to one another, tender-hearted, forgiving one another, as God in Christ forgave you. Ephesians 4:32 (ESV)

▷ **Have YOU ever had to ask a friend to forgive you? Was it hard?**

▷ **Have you ever had to forgive a friend for something he or she did to YOU? Was that harder or easier than asking for forgiveness?**

CHAPTER TEN

"Micah?"

"Armin?"

"Lydia?"

"That's the thief?"

"A possum?"

"Gabe's pet possum?"

The questions piled one on top of another as Micah, Armin, and Lydia all talked excitedly at the same time. Bit by bit they pieced the whole story together. Armin and Lydia, it turned out, had been following similar clues to Micah's and ended up in the basement only to find Micah staring at a possum on top of a pile of sketchbook paper and one right shoe. Once they saw that, everything fell right into place.

How did they know it was a pet possum and not just some wild possum off the streets? Because it happened to have a collar and a name tag.

And how did they know it was Gabe's pet possum? Because who else in the greater Middletown area would be weird enough to have a pet possum? With its pointy, rat-like nose, its sharp little teeth, and its beady little eyes, this was truly a creature only a Gabe could love.

They stood there staring at the ugly beast, not sure what to do next. It didn't look like something you'd want to pick up and cuddle.

Micah took advantage of the silence. "Listen, Armin, I'm really sorry about the way I've been treating this whole mystery. I wasn't really taking it seriously. I realize now how important this sketchbook was to you."

"It's okay, Micah. I've been thinking too. My

sketchbook was important because it had a lot of pictures that really mattered to me—including drawings of my friends. But do you know what's even more important than drawings of my friends?"

"What?" Micah asked.

"My friends!"

"Wow. That was really corny!" said Lydia. But she said it with a smile. "But just so you know, I'm sorry for being a wet blanket during the investigation. It turns out you two really can figure a few things out now and then!"

"Okay, if we're all getting things off our chest, I have one more confession," said Armin.

"What's that?"

"I know solving this crime was probably more important to me than to either of you two, but I have to admit—Micah was right. It was also really fun!"

"All we have to do next is figure out how to get this hideous creature back to Gabe."

Armin nodded. "If you two stay here, I'll try to find him."

Armin turned around to head back toward the stairs, when all of a sudden, the possum darted off toward a shadowy corner.

"Too late!" shouted Micah. "Armin, we need your help!"

The race was on! All three kids took off in the direction of the possum. But just as they were on the verge of catching up to it, it shot away to its next hiding spot, behind pipes or shelves or other odds and ends in the huge basement. There seemed to be an unending supply of things to hide behind. The good news was, their eyes had adjusted by this time, so it was much easier to see the animal move back and forth and chase it to its next spot.

It didn't take long before they realized their strategy was getting them nowhere. They decided to split up, each rushing at the pesky pet from a different side. Micah thought he had a perfect angle on the possum in a corner behind an old ladder, when quick as lightning, it dodged around him and headed toward the stairs.

"To the kitchen!" Micah shouted.

The gray possum looked like a little rain cloud being blown across the basement floor and then up the steps. It was amazing how quickly that creature could run on its tiny little possum legs.

The kids all rushed after it as quick as their regular-size legs would carry them. Up they went, Micah, then Lydia, then Armin. Just as Micah got to the top of the stairs and pushed the basement door open, he caught a glimpse of the possum darting out of the swinging kitchen doors and into the lunchroom on the other side.

The three kids rushed into the lunchroom.

"There he is!" Armin shouted, pointing into the corner on their left. Armin and Lydia rushed right at him, but Micah curved around in front to block off his exit. He figured it was time to outsmart the possum.

It turned out, it wasn't so easy. The creature shot right between them and rushed toward the big, open doors between the lunchroom and the lobby. By the time they got out to the lobby, the possum was nowhere to be seen.

But he was somewhere to be heard.

To be precise, Micah didn't hear the possum itself. He heard the shrieks and screams of terrified children in the auditorium. But it was easy to put two and two together.

As Micah, Armin, and Lydia rushed through the lobby, they could hear Mr. Turtell, still at the ticket table, mumbling to himself. "Or maybe it's about how all the honeybees have disappeared. Or the way cantaloupe always smells like rotten fruit, even when it's fresh."

"What's he talking about?" Armin asked Micah as they pushed through the auditorium doors.

"I'll explain later."

Micah glanced around the auditorium and could barely believe his eyes. It looked as crazy in there as it had sounded from outside the doors. Kids half-dressed in vegetable costumes were running this way and that, screaming their heads off like the end of the world was on its way.

"What is it?"

"It's going to bite us!"

"It's going to eat us!"

"It's got fangs!"

"It's a vampire cat!"

"It's a ghost hamster!"

"It's a zombie rat!"

That last explanation must have seemed the most logical, especially among the kindergartners. Soon they were all running up and down the aisles, screaming "Zombie rat! Zombie rat!" Some of them tried climbing the curtains or the catwalk ladder or anything else they could climb to get away from the strange creature haunting the ground. But almost as soon as they started up, someone else started shouting, "It can climb! It can climb!" Immediately everyone scrambled back down.

No one knew how to escape, so they ran every which way and bounced up and down like bits of popcorn heating in a pan.

Miss Petunia, Mrs. Millwood, and a handful

of other moms and dads tried their best to restore order. But every time they managed to calm some kids down, the possum would run by and leave them in a panic once again.

The only one who truly remained calm was Gabe. He stood onstage, watching his pet run back and forth. "Here, Burt! Come here, Burt! I'm so glad I found you! Where have you been?"

But "Burt" (which was apparently the possum's name) did not come when called. Either he was as scared of the kids as they were of him, or he was having the time of his life chasing them around and riling them up. Either way, the possum didn't seem to be stopping any time soon.

At this point Micah, Armin, and Lydia were also running around in the chaos, but instead of running away from the zombie rat, they were running toward it. After several laps up and down the auditorium aisles, they managed to chase it up onto the stage toward Gabe. But instead of stopping to say hello to its owner, the possum darted past him behind the curtain.

Micah and Lydia shook the curtains to see if they could flush Burt out while Armin rushed behind to see if he'd slipped out the back. "There he goes!" Armin shouted, pointing toward the back hallway by the dressing rooms.

All four of them—including Gabe—rushed to the right of the stage to see Burt running down the long hallway like a rat who'd finally caught a glimpse of its cheese at the end of a maze. The possum was running straight toward what must have looked like a tall, green tree, but was, in fact, a stalk of celery.

But not just any celery—the lead celery.

"Ahhhhh!" Hanz screamed, waving his arms in front of him to ward off the zombie rat.

But the possum didn't even slow down. As fast as its little legs would carry him, he charged the tree and shot up into its branches, climbing all the way to the green, leafy top.

And there he sat, looking altogether comfortable in what must have seemed like his natural environment.

"Get it off me! Get it off me!" Hanz shouted. "Vy is it doing zis? It's going to bite my ears off, and zen it's going to eat on my nose!"

"Don't worry," said Gabe. "He doesn't bite."

With both hands he reached up into the green, felt leaves at the top of Hanz's celery costume.

"Ouch!" Gabe shouted, then shrugged. "I guess I was wrong."

Gabe held up his left thumb. Two small beads of blood were forming on the knuckle.

Micah caught a glimpse of Hanz out of the corner of his eye, staring at the bleeding thumb. His face now looked as green as his celery costume. "Zat's vat vill happen to my ears and my—"

But he never finished his sentence. Instead, his eyes glazed over and he fell down backward, like a tree chopped down in the woods.

"He fainted!" Micah said. "And look at Burt! Is he dead?"

The possum lay on his back with his legs in the air.

Gabe shook his head. "No, he's just pretending. I think the fall startled him."

"Quick! Grab that bag!" said Lydia.

Armin grabbed an empty backpack lying in the hallway and handed it to Lydia. Lydia grabbed Burt by the tail and tossed him inside as quick as she could. Then she zipped it up and handed it to Gabe.

"Thanks!" he said. "Boy, I sure did miss him."

Micah, Lydia, and Armin just looked at one another and shrugged.

"You should probably have that bite looked at," said Lydia.

Gabe nodded. "I hope I don't have to get another round of shots."

The Ole Act is Back

We did it! I feel like I'm on top of the world! Just yesterday it felt like we'd never come together as a team and have a good performance, but tonight we did it!

I am so proud of what we accomplishedt onstage, but I'm even more excited that me, Armin, and Lydia are all friends again. We've come through quite a rough patch, but I think it made us stronger than ever.

Let that be a lesson to all the art thieves . . . er, possums of the world. You may be able to tear up our sketchbooks, but you can never tear our friendship apart! Hey, that's almost poetic. Which reminds me: I should start working on my cop show theme song.

Two are better than one, because they have a good return for their labor: If either of them falls down, one can help the other up.
Ecclesiastes 4:9-10 (NIV)

▷ **Have YOU ever worked together with a group to do something amazing that you could have never done on your own?**

▷ **How can YOU be someone others can rely on in a time of need?**

CHAPTER ELEVEN

After handing Burt over to Gabe's mom, Gabe, Micah, Armin, and Lydia had to hurry to get in their costumes and makeup before the play started. Luckily, Mrs. Millwood was ready for them, and in just a few minutes' time, Gabe looked like a gummy worm, Micah was green, Armin was red, and Lydia was a creamy tan. (Which really wasn't much of a change for Lydia.)

That night, as they listened from backstage, waiting for their chance to perform, Micah felt almost like he was hearing the play for the very first time. "You know, this play is kinda growing on me."

"Yeah," Armin agreed. "It's pretty deep. It takes a while to catch all the layers."

Lydia rolled her eyes. "You two still don't know what it's about, do you?"

"Maybe not," Micah said. "But that doesn't mean we don't appreciate it."

Armin nodded. "Yeah. It's just like Philosophical Haircut's song lyrics. No one knows what they mean. You just have to let their deepness wash over you."

"Whatever."

"Speaking of deepness," Micah said, "It's almost time for us to be onstage for our big scene!"

They stood there, waiting in nervous silence for several minutes, until finally the band cued up their entrance song. Out they marched, taking the stage with confidence and poise. They were in a much better place than the night before, and this time they knew they'd nail it!

And nail it they did!

For the most part.

Micah only tripped once, and he didn't mess up

more than three or four lines. All in all, a banner performance!

Meanwhile, Lydia was perfect, as usual. And no one could dance like Armin. In fact, all the foods in act 2 did a remarkable job speaking their lines with conviction and enthusiasm. Whether they understood the play or not, they sure sounded like they did! From top to bottom, it was an amazing performance!

Micah and his friends weren't in act 3 until the very last scene of the play. In that scene, all thirty-two cast members had to be onstage at the same time, singing and dancing the grand finale. They lined up straight across the stage, with their arms on the shoulders of the person next to them, kicking their legs in the air like those Rockette dancers at the Thanksgiving Day parade in New York.

About a third of the time they'd practiced that number, one or two of the dancers would lose their balance and fall, which under normal circumstances is no big deal. But when everyone is linked together, arms around shoulders, it can be chaos. When one person goes down, everybody goes down. It's a domino effect that ends in a heaping pile of children all over the floor.

Of course, the opening night's grand finale had turned out that way—with all the mishaps of the night, a heaping pile of children on the floor made perfect sense. In fact, most of the people in the audience assumed the collapse of the dancers was on purpose. It fit the dark tone of the rest of the play.

Ah, but it was never meant to be this way. So, on this final night of the production, all the performers were hoping for perfection! Or at least they were hoping to end up still on their feet. So, when the band started playing and they linked together, they crossed their fingers and hoped for the best.

And they looked terrific! All the weird foods kicked and swung together in a perfect line. Just as Miss Petunia had foretold, they became the biggest smorgasbord in the history of live theater!

Ah, but such things weren't meant to last. With Armin on his right and Lydia on his left, Micah was belting out the lyrics as loud as he could. He was completely lost in the music when one of his dance kicks went wrong. His left boot started to slip. He tried to adjust his weight, but it only slipped further.

In a panic, he realized he was about to go down. And he was going to take the whole line down with him. The last song would be ruined, and it was all his fault!

But then, all of a sudden, he felt himself floating above the stage! The shoulders beside him—Armin's and Lydia's, had caught him just before he went down. And then, without a word, they held him up until he could get his feet back under him.

All was well. The song ended, and they took a huge bow. What a rush!

And you know what? A small part of him even felt like he'd done as Miss Petunia had hoped: he'd transformed, becoming the very essence of an artichoke. Whatever that meant.

Hold Your Applause

What a night! It was a rush to hear all that applause and to know I was a part of something that a crowd really enjoyed. I'm not used to being this successful. Don't worry—I won't let it go to my head.

But seriously, I know applause doesn't last very long, and then you have to move on and do your best at the next thing. I'm learning that just doing your best is the most important thing. It sure is fun to do well and please others, but it's even better to please God.

And the truth is, God is looking at the inner me rather than the outer me. Which is good, because the outer me is often covered in mismatched socks and bedhead hair and food stains from breakfast and . . . well, you get the idea.

Whatever you do, work heartily, as for the Lord and not for men.
Colossians 3:23 (ESV)

▷ **Have YOU ever gotten an award or a trophy for doing something well? How did it feel?**

▷ **What are some ways YOU can please God in the daily things you do?**

CHAPTER TWELVE

Micah got out of his costume, washed off his makeup, and went out to the lobby to meet his family. His mom gave him a huge hug as soon as he walked through the door.

"That was amazing! You were incredible!"

"Well . . . I still missed a few lines here and there," Micah admitted, trying to downplay his success. Still, he was grinning ear to ear.

"No, you really were terrific!" said his dad. "The whole cast was! And it was so much more . . . upbeat than last night's performance."

"Yeah, it really was!" said his mom. "It was

cheerful! Hopeful! You guys seemed to be having a great time!"

"Thanks. We fixed a few things that weren't quite right yesterday." Micah didn't feel like going into more detail than this. He was just happy that they were happy.

Audrey, who had been sulking in a corner with some of her friends, noticed Micah and came over. "What happened?" she asked. "Last night's show was so good, and tonight was terrible! Where was the rage? The angst? The unsettling commentary on the plight of modern man?!?"

She glared at him one more time, then stomped off in a huff.

"What was that all about?" Micah's mom asked.

His dad shrugged. "I guess last night's performance was more teen-friendly."

On Monday, Micah, Armin, and Lydia soaked up every ounce of the play's success. The reviews had come in Sunday's papers, and everyone was raving!

All day long, the whole cast received compliment after compliment on their singing, dancing, and acting. Even Mr. Turtell, who was still trying to work out what the play was all about, had to admit he was emotionally moved by the performances.

"I'm not one to cry," he'd told their class, "so I didn't. But if I were one to cry, I probably would have."

He'd never spoken so highly of a musical in his entire life.

Review of *Don't You Carrot All?* in the Middletown Gazette

Saturday night at New Leaf Elementary, audience members were treated to an incredible performance of Annabelle Petunia's latest food-based musical, "Don't You Carrot All?"

The actors embodied their roles like none I've ever seen. From the amazing bond of friendship between the artichoke, the box of raisins, and the cream of mushroom soup, to the excruciating pain on the face of the lead celery–it's hard to imagine more realistic portrayals of food emotions!

It can be difficult to capture such an intricate and complex work of art in mere words. Is it about capitalism? Possibly. Animal rights? Maybe. The death of polka music? Probably not. But what it was mostly about was friendship. Friendships that cross barriers. Friendships that last through good times and bad.

After last season's production of Miss Petunia's "Something to Taco 'Bout," I thought she had come to the end of her run with food-based plays. What else was there to say? But after watching this smashing success of a show, I'm rethinking my position. May her food-based productions never end!

At recess Micah sat on a swing next to Armin and Lydia.

"I heard people say that was one of the best plays in school history!" Micah announced.

Armin agreed. "Or at least one of the best food-based plays!"

Lydia nodded. "It was definitely the best vegetarian food-based play!"

Chet walked up to them with a kindergartner's head sticking out of his armpit, in perfect noogie position. "Did you nerds ever catch the kid who stole your stuff?"

"Actually," Micah told him, "it turned out to be a possum."

"Gabe's pet possum," said Armin.

Chet gave the kindergartner a quick noogie and sent him on his way. "I'm glad to hear it. I wasn't too thrilled about some other criminal crowding in on my turf! But I'm cool with possums."

Armin shrugged. "Who isn't?"

Meanwhile, out of the corner of his eye, Micah

caught a glimpse of Gabe crawling around on his belly under the monkey bars. "What do you think he's doing?"

"Hey Gabe!" Armin shouted.

Gabe looked up at them in surprise. "Oh, hey guys!

"The play's over," Lydia told him. "You know you don't have to act like a gummy worm anymore."

But suddenly Micah wondered—maybe he wasn't crawling around for fun. Maybe he was looking for something down there.

Micah walked to the monkey bars. "Something I can help you with?"

"Did you happen to see my pet snake anywhere around here?"

As a Matter of Fact . . .

Who would have thought one of Miss Petunia's weird, food-based productions would be such a hit? I never imagined I'd have such a great time performing—or more amazingly, do a good job!

But you know, I would have been fine however the play ended up as long as me and my friends worked things out. I'm so glad things are back to normal between us. I am so thankful for the friends God has given me, and that He keeps our friendship strong even when we screw it up.

We went through a tough spot, but in the end it all worked out for the best. We learned a few things during our quest to catch the sketchbook thief:

BELIEVE THE BEST

When we have disagreements (and we will have them), we need to be patient and kind with each other. Good friends believe the best about each other and always take the time to find out the truth.

BE QUICK TO FORGIVE

When we mess up, we should be quick to forgive, just like God is quick to forgive us when we ask Him to. We all make mistakes. Real friends are good at making things right.

Miss Petunia's play title was a bit ironic considering what was going on behind the scenes. Don't You Carrot All? As a matter of fact, I do. I care a whole lot!

Above all, keep loving one another earnestly, since love covers a multitude of sins.
1 Peter 4:8 (ESV)

▷ **How can YOU say thanks to your friends when they are there for you?**

▷ **Can YOU think of ways to make your friendships even stronger than they are now?**

About the Author

Andy McGuire has written and illustrated four children's books, including *Remy the Rhino* and *Rainy Day Games*. He has a BA in creative writing from Miami University and an MA in literature from Ohio University. Andy's writing heroes have always been the ones who make him laugh, from Roald Dahl and Louis Sachar to P. G. Wodehouse and William Goldman. Andy lives with his wife and three children in Burnsville, Minnesota.

About the Illustrator

Girish Manuel is the creator of the Micah's Super Vlog video series and a producer at Square One World Media. He lives in a little place called Winnipeg, Canada, with his lovely wife, Nikki, and furry cat, Paska. Girish enjoys running and drawing . . . but not at the same time. That would be hard. He tried it once and got ink all over his shoes.

Have you ever felt like you couldn't do anything right?

We all do stuff that we shouldn't do.

Maybe we've told a lie, or even stolen something...

When we go our own way instead of God's, it's called **SIN**.

Sin keeps us from being close to God and it has some other serious consequences...

but I've got some good news!

GOD LOVES YOU!

°Yes, the amazing, incredible, Creator who made the universe and everything in it (including YOU) loves you!

How do I know this?

Because God is my friend. And He wants to be your friend too!

Check this out:

When we sin, the payment is death (Romans 6:23). But God gives us the gift of eternal life (John 3:16). That's because of what Jesus did for us on the cross.

What did Jesus do exactly?

Jesus, God's very own Son, came down to earth to save us from our sin and restore our relationship with God! He did that by living a perfect life (without sin!) and taking the punishment for OUR sins when He was nailed to a cross (a punishment for really bad criminals back then)!

Jesus did this because He loved us enough to take OUR punishment! But that's not the end of the story. Three days after His death, Jesus rose from the grave, proving that God has power over sin and death!

So, what now?

Even though there's countless things we have done wrong, God can forgive our sins ... no matter how many or how big they are! He wants to have a relationship with you through Jesus!

Check this out:

Everyone sins (Romans 3:23). No one measures up to God's glory. But God's free gift of grace makes us right with Him. Jesus paid the price to set us free!

How?

Even though we can't do anything to save ourselves from sin, we can be saved because of what Jesus has already done! By trusting Him with your life, you can live free from guilt and shame, knowing that YOU ARE LOVED!

If you're ready to accept God's gift and live LOVED, simply pray this prayer:

Dear Jesus, thank You for loving me and dying on the cross for my sins. Today I accept God's gift of salvation and I invite You to be the King of my heart. Please forgive me of my sins and guide me as I grow in friendship with You. Jesus, I want to be more like You and share Your love with others. Thank You that I don't have to be perfect but can grow in faith as I follow Your ways. In Your name I pray, amen

FIND ARMIN'S SKETCHBOOK!

CHECK OUT OTHER BOOKS ABOUT MICAH AND HIS FRIENDS!

MICAH'S GOT TALENT?
BY ANDY MCGUIRE
ILLUSTRATED BY GIRISH MANUEL

THE BIG FAIL
BY ANDY MCGUIRE
ILLUSTRATED BY GIRISH MANUEL

TO SKETCH A THIEF
BY ANDY MCGUIRE
ILLUSTRATED BY GIRISH MANUEL

JUST CHILL
BY ANDY MCGUIRE
ILLUSTRATED BY GIRISH MANUEL

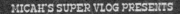